A Harmless Little Ruse

(Harmless Series №2)

by Meli Raine

She has no idea what she's doing. Loose cannons never hit their targets.

And they take out plenty of collateral damage.

Four years ago Lindsay experienced the unspeakable right before me, and I couldn't stop them.

But that's all changed now.

When her father, Senator Bosworth, contacted me to ask — demand — that I protect her, it was a second chance. A shot at redemption.

An opportunity to right an unspeakable wrong.

Controlling Lindsay as she seeks her revenge on the monsters who hurt her won't be hard.

Containing my own out-of-control feelings for Lindsay and keeping up this ruse of cold-blooded distance will be.

Even harder than admitting to her what really happened that night four years ago.

It turns out I don't have to, though.

Someone else did it for me.

And I'll make sure they regret it.

* * *

A Harmless Little Ruse is the second book in this political thriller/romantic suspense trilogy by USA Today bestselling author Meli Raine, and is entirely from Drew's perspective.

Join my New Releases and Sales newsletter at: http://eepurl.com/beV0gf

Author's note: I also write romantic comedy as Julia Kent and paranormal shifter romance as one-half of the writing duo Diana Seere. Check out those books as well. ;)

CHAPTER ONE

I wake up to an empty bed.
It's not mine.

Lindsay's gone.

I can feel a change in the air. I jump to my feet, instantly alert, blood pumping to arms and legs that are battle-ready. Her bedroom room smells like lavender and beeswax, mingled with the hot scent of sex. I swear her heat still lingers on the sheets. The ceiling fan is still, the room crackling with silence.

I grab my gun belt and --

What the hell?

My weapon is missing.

Gun's gone.

Lindsay's gone.

Oh, shit.

She didn't?

She did.

"Gentian," I bark as I shove my earpiece in. "Where's Lilac?" Lilac's her code name.

"With you," he responds.

"Negative."

Dead air.

"Gentian?"

"I don't know, sir. No one's seen her. Last we knew, she was locked in her bedroom with you."

No trace of irony. No hint of teasing. If he had even one whiff of either, he'd have his ass handed to him.

And he knows it.

"She's gone, Gentian. Find her."

"Yes, sir."

A Harmless Little Ruse

The instant flurry of activity in the house matches my organs. They rearrange themselves inside me as I assess the situation, which is pretty fucking simple.

Lindsay stole my gun and ran away.

Doesn't get much simpler than that.

Last night was the first time in four damn years that I slept. Actual REM sleep. The night those bastards tortured us was the first night of my new life.

A life without sleep.

And last night?

I slept like someone who had finally come home.

"Jesus," I mutter to myself. "Great job, Drew. She totally snowed you."

I have to hand it to Lindsay. She fooled me. I believed her act the entire time. She managed to outwit us all.

Damn smart woman.

Damn dangerous, too.

A thousand points of information flood my mind. My job is to sort out the unimportant details, laser in on what's significant, and create an instant plan from that.

Only one man is better than me in a situation like this.

Lucky for me, he's a phone call away, and on my payroll.

Speed dial is my friend.

" 'lo?" Mark Paulson's sleepy voice answers the phone, and before I can say a word, he goes into full alert mode. "Paulson here. What do you need, Drew?"

Now that's a soldier.

"My detail stole my weapon and escaped."

Silence.

Yeah, I'm going to pay for this by being mocked for years.

"She *what*?"

"You heard me."

More silence.

"Give me half an hour. I'll be there."

Click.

A few months ago, Mark called me in on a complicated mission to rescue his kidnapped girlfriend, Carrie. Ex-DEA, ex-Special Ops, and probably ex-secret agencies even Senator Bosworth doesn't know about, Paulson has the most strategic mind I've ever seen. He's like a chess grandmaster combined with a ruthless mercenary.

Which makes him my second in command at my private security company.

He's second in name only, though. Called in only for extreme missions, Paulson's trying to lay low and recover from the hell of having his woman nearly chopped into pieces and enjoyed by one of the most perverted drug and sex slave smugglers in U.S. history.

But enough about that.

Lindsay just stole my gun and ran away.

"Fuck." The truth of it starts to sink in. I anchor myself with facts.

Fact: that gun is not registered, has no ID number, and cannot be tracked back to me.

Fact: the three targets who defiled her four years ago are texting and taunting her.

Fact: the three targets tried to kill her with her own car.

Fact: she managed to escape a perimeter set up with nine of the best military-trained security guys in the world.

Fact: I can still taste her on my tongue.

"Sir?" Gentian walks into the room with a hard, tight face. "We found tracks in the...." His voice drops off as his eyes travel to my throat. He stares.

I look down.

The tag of my t-shirt sticks out. I've put my shirt on backwards and inside out.

So much for pretense.

"Did something happen between you and Lindsay last night, sir?" His eyes go dark.

"What do you think?" He's treading on very dangerous territory now.

"Did she run away because of you, *sir*?" His point is crystal clear.

Before I can punch him, impulse control kicks in. I plant my hands on my hips, take in a deep breath, and start to laugh.

It's a bitter sound.

I've trained him well. He's putting the client's welfare ahead of pleasing his boss.

Good man.

"Nothing happened between us that would cause her to steal my weapon and run away."

Gentian's eyes fly wide open. "Your weapon?"

"Yeah."

He knows better than to react further. "Is that confidential?"

"For now."

"Is she unstable?"

He's really asking whether she'll shoot anyone on our security detail.

"No. She has a specific target."

"More than one?"

Damn, he's smarter than he looks.

"I suspect she's going after her attackers from four years ago."

"I sure would."

That's the first hint of unprofessionalism out of him.

"What you would or would not do if you were in the client's shoes has no bearing on what you're going to do right now, Gentian."

"Yes, sir."

"Expand the perimeter search. Disable all vehicles on the grounds. Check for hitchhikers. Call gun stores and alert them to anyone buying bullets that match my weapon."

Someone speaks into his headset. Gentian murmurs back, then tells me, "All vehicles accounted for."

Cold steel shoots through my gut. Good news.

"Then she's on foot. Get as many guys in the field as you can." I ignore the shoreline below. No way she got her hands on a boat. She knows how to jet ski and that's it. Lindsay wouldn't --

Wait.

The Lindsay I knew four years ago wouldn't.

The woman I'm dealing with *now*?

Who the hell knows.

"Done." Gentian speaks into his earpiece, then turns to me and asks, "Do we inform Senator Bosworth and Mrs. Bosworth?"

That cold steel in my gut turns into hot metal.

I rake my hand through my hair. My fingers smell like her. Smell like sex and fun and smiles and groans. Like freedom.

Like reclaiming.

And she fucking threw it away for revenge.

"Sir?"

I shake it off. "No. Not yet. Containment on all levels. Get her roped in, get this situation under control, and we'll reassess if we can't locate her quickly. Timeline silence."

"Yes, sir."

"And I want tails on all three of the targets."

"Already done."

"Add one more each."

"Yes, sir." Gentian's mouth sets in a firm line. He knows how bad this is.

How bad this is for Lindsay.

How bad this is for *me*.

"And check her phone records."

He nods. He leaves.

I breathe. At least, I try.

And then I let a tiny bit of emotional pressure out. Just a few seconds' worth. If I don't, I'll explode, and you can't be strategic and emotional at the same time.

You fail all around.

"What are you doing, Lindsay?" I mutter to myself, pacing the room like a caged animal. The room is stripped clean, devoid of any real personality. What personal effects she has are from four years ago. Adele posters on the walls, an old iPhone from 2012, and concert tickets littering a bulletin board, stopping nearly four years ago at the month of the attack.

Lindsay's used me to get her hands on a gun, so she can kill John, Stellan and Blaine. She's a loose cannon.

And loose cannons never hit their targets.

CHAPTER TWO

I run through last night over and over. No part of the intimacy stands out as fake. She wasn't faking those moans, her sighs, her beautiful orgasms, her crying at the end, her acceptance of my comfort and my love.

"That was *not* an act," I hiss under my breath, grabbing a bed pillow and throwing it at the window. It sails through, the thin sheer curtain billowing through the opening. I punch a second pillow so hard it flies across the bed and lands on top of her alarm clock, knocking it off the nightstand.

"You think you're fooling me," I say to no one, arms tense, shoulders tight as rocks, my mind racing. "But you're not *this* Lindsay. You're not. No way you changed that much."

The emotional impact of what she's done feels like the wind's been knocked out of me. She did this. She *really* did this. She opened up to me last night and we connected. We more than connected. We reveled and we healed and we --

"FUCK!" I scream, remembering how much I needed to please her last night, how she healed in my arms. I felt it. I didn't imagine it.

We cracked open the door to the future. We pried the nails from that closed-off door. One by one, we did it.

And she just dumped an entire cement mixer's load of concrete on top of it.

Protectiveness pumps through my veins like adrenaline mixed with caffeine and uppers. My pulse is in my cock, my tongue, my throat. She's out there, alone, thinking she's smarter than my entire team of guys who were hired to make sure no one ever hurts her again.

I push aside the question of who *she* hurts. Let's not go there.

Not now.

A Harmless Little Ruse

"Jesus, Lindsay, are you out of your mind?" I'm talking to myself again.

Sheer speculation makes my mind fill with worst-case scenarios. The world is dangerous enough. Add three well-connected psychopaths with a penchant for playing Cat and Mouse, and danger seems like a preschool playground.

Lindsay's put herself in mortal peril.

Whether she likes it or not, I have to get her out.

Those crazy assholes are out for blood.

And more.

I peer out the open window and look at the pillow, caught in the tree branches right outside her window. A cat meows. Again. *Again.*

I tense.

Something's off.

My body's half in, half out of the window. A light breeze pushes the leaves toward me, the rustle a familiar sound. When you live this close to the ocean, the wind becomes a second language.

And it's telling me something right now.

Instinct takes over. The amygdala sends rat-brain signals to my body. I stand up on the windowsill, look down, and coil my leg muscles. Too tight and I'll snap a bone. Too loose and I'll burst my spleen.

And...I jump.

You think the impact from the landing is the worst part of a long fall. It's actually the seconds where you're suspended in midair. With nothing to set you in space and time, you float.

You float like there is no sense of touch. Reaching out yields air. You can't track time or measure your space. It's like you don't exist.

Until you land.

I dart to the left, my thighs screaming from quick, sharp movement.

I tackle the sound before I even hear it. My arms whip around the source of the noise, caging it in, pressing it against the mulch and grass, the carefully edged lawn around the base of the house.

"Mphhhh! Mmmm! Uh uh!" says the sound.

The sound is soft and hot, twisty and frantic.

And then the sound speaks.

"Fuck you, Drew!"

I sigh, as much as you can sigh while you're taking an adrenaline bath as you straddle the woman who stole your gun and escaped from nine members of your security team.

"I love you, too, Lindsay."

"Let me go!"

"No."

"You can't keep me here."

She's legally right, but operationally wrong.

I lighten up just enough for her to move from her side onto her back, our mouths inches apart.

Just like a few hours ago, in her bed.

A few pesky little details have changed since then.

"Where's my gun?"

She clamps her lips shut.

Like *that's* going to work.

"Lindsay," I say in a low, even voice that is designed to scare the shit out of her. "Give me my gun or I'll have my guys personally escort you back to that fucking island, only this time you'll arrive by parachute in the ocean a quarter mile offshore."

She snorts. "You wouldn't."

The ragged, excited breaths she's taking make her loose breasts push up against my chest, over and over. Our nipples brush up against each other.

Both sets are hard.

So is something else.

On me.

"Try me. You stole my firearm," I hiss. "What the fuck were you thinking? Do you have any idea how dangerous that is? And what are you planning to do?" In the moonlight, her eyes should be big as saucers, frightened and agitated.

But they're narrow and calculating.

Like a cat.

"You think you can escape and go get John, Stellan and Blaine? You stupid little -- "

The bite comes out of nowhere as she sits up, her core muscles so fucking powerful she bucks me up an inch or so, and she's biting my ear.

I see stars.

But I'm not getting off her. She's driven me to this extreme.

The only way to protect Lindsay is to literally pin her in place with my body.

And there are two ways we can do this.

The hard way

or

The harder way

So I headbutt her.

I see stars again, but she lets go and squeals, then howls in pain.

"Why did you *dooooo* that?" she moans, pressing the bridge of her nose with her fingers, rocking in place.

Ignoring her version of *please*, I get off her. She won't bite me like that again. I haul her up and use an arm-twist technique that immobilizes her.

"Gun."

"I don't know what you're talking about." She juts her chin up, defiant.

God, she's so fucking rebellious and hot.

And a pain in the ass.

"You can be charged with multiple felonies for stealing a firearm from an active-duty military officer and a federal -- "

"Prove it."

"Prove you stole my gun?" I snort. "Your fingerprints are all over it." She's twisting in my hands but there's no hope. I've held guys three times her size with this technique.

"Prove the gun exists."

Wasn't expecting *that*.

"Prove the *what*?"

"It's not registered. All the metal's been filed down. Bet it's untraceable. Which means I can't steal something that doesn't exist, Drew," she says, taunting me.

Teasing me.

Blood runs in a small trickle from her left nostril, looking like a black worm in the night.

"Do you mind?" She jostles her hands. "Can I wipe my nose that *you* just injured? Daddy is going to shit a brick when he finds out you've abused his daughter."

"And when he finds out you stole my gun to go after three well-established, highly successful men to fulfill some sick, mentally unbalanced scheme you have for revenge against guys who did nothing more than meet your request for some gang bang sex, I don't think your version of events is the one he's going to believe."

She moves to kick me in the balls.

I'm a nanosecond faster and swoop my foot across her ankles.

Lindsay drops. I let go of her wrist.

"You bastard," she says from the ground, looking up at me, blood smeared and eyes wide and feral now.

"You think this is me being a bastard, Lindsay? Really? Because on a scale of bastard, this is downright courtly."

"You bruise me and headbutt me and give me a bloody nose and you call that *courtly*?"

"You pretend to want me, give me a little intimacy -- " My voice cracks on that word, damn it. "And then steal my gun and try to escape. You really aren't in a position to demand anything from me behavior-wise."

Her lips purse, nostrils flaring, and she grabs the hem of her shirt, pulling it up to wipe her nose.

A flash of dusky nipples greets my gaze.

I bite back a groan.

We're both panting, angry, frustrated, feeling betrayed, and turned on as *fuck*.

Or maybe that's just me.

"Lindsay. Give me my gun. I'm not going to stop asking."

She plants the soles of her feet on the ground. She's wearing black leather sneakers, black sweatpants, a black hoodie with a black t-shirt underneath.

Who does she think she is? An Emo ninja?

Her head dips between her knees and she just breathes.

Footsteps. Leaves rustling. And then --

"Sir?"

It's Gentian.

"Call them off. Found her."

He eyes me uncertainly. "And your -- "

"And nothing. Target found. Do the rest."

"Yes, sir." Gentian runs off.

A Harmless Little Ruse

"You are just like Daddy," Lindsay says, contempt so thick in her voice I could wear it as sunscreen in Afghanistan and stay pasty white. "You think you can order everyone around and they'll do your bidding like good little robots. I spent four years of my life on that island because Daddy made his mission more important than me."

"*My* mission would be easier if you were just a robot." My damn erection taunts me. Wish *I* were a robot right now.

"This mission wouldn't exist if I were dead."

I explode. "That's the point, Lindsay! My job is to keep you undead!"

"Your job is to turn me into a zombie?" She gives me a withering look.

I ignore that. "Where's my gun?"

"What gun?"

I grab her arm, hard. My fingertips dig into her wiry muscles. I know I'm hurting her. A sick little corner of me enjoys hurting her. I can't admit it, but she fucking *gutted* me back in her bedroom, letting me wake up like that. Alone. Used.

A mark for her sick little game. Is that all this is?

She squirms, but juts her chin up at me, defiant, glaring.

I dare you, those honey-brown eyes say, turning dark as this standoff continues.

Oh, yeah?

I don't back down.

Ever.

Pain enters those eyes, then fear. Good. A healthy dose of fear means we're getting somewhere. She should be afraid. Not of me. Of *them*.

Any fear, though, is progress.

"Let go."

"My gun."

She nudges her chin toward the bush behind me. I push her toward it.

"Get it."

"How can I get it when you're squeezing me like a nut in a wrench?"

"You got the 'nut' part right."

She scowls, then rolls her eyes.

I'd laugh if I were in a different mood, but now I'm pissed. Not so much about the gun, which was bad.

Pissed that she left me like that.

And by pissed, I mean *hurt*.

"You are such an asshole. How can I bend over when you're holding me like this?"

I reach up for her hair with my free hand and snake my fingers through it, threading it like a Chinese finger torture puzzle through my knuckles.

"What are you doing?"

I let go of her upper arm.

She bolts.

Then yanks back with such force I have to lean down slightly or I'll rip all her hair out at the roots because of the sheer force of *her* movement.

Her scream dies in her throat.

"You bastard," she gasps, pooled at my feet into a panting little ball of hard, tight anger. Her chest rises and falls and God help me, my blood goes where it shouldn't. I need all the oxygen to go to my brain. Last thing my pants need is a tent.

"I may be a bastard, but I'm not a sucker, Lindsay. Bend down and find my gun."

"You just want me to bend down so you can see my ass."

I stay silent, because one of the rules of handling a hostile person is to give them something to be right about.

I can give her a victory on that topic.

Because she is mostly correct.

It's not the only reason, but it's a nice fringe benefit.

Five seconds later, my gun's in my waistband, and she's two feet away from me. I let her go.

We're at an impasse.

"Just let me leave, Drew. I'll disappear. Run away. Hide. I know how." Her voice is so contrite. Her pleading is damn close to begging. These mood swings are killing me.

Why the change in her? What's made her so desperate to leave?

"You think letting a presidential candidate's daughter escape to go live an underground life is on my list of Shit I Want to Do Tonight?" I start laughing. It's not a pleasant sound. "You're as crazy as your parents think you are, Lindsay!"

She winces. I hurt her. Hit a nerve. Her eyes simmer in the moonlight, unspilled tears pooling on her lower lids. As pissed as I am, I regret that comment. My heart starts doing the two-step in my chest, and my hands curl into fists so I don't reach out and pull her into my arms and whisper *I'm sorry*.

If I do that, it's like handing her a scalpel and telling her to cut out my beating heart and use it as a metronome.

"Plus," I add, "whatever you think you know about disappearing is nothing compared to how much more the people who want to get their hands on you know about it. You'd be tracked, found, kidnapped and dead – or worse – before you know it."

She shudders at the word *worse*.

Footsteps.

"Help!" Lindsay starts screaming.

"What are you doing?" I plant my hands on my hips and just watch, unamused.

"I'm going to tell Silas what you did to me."

I snort. "You mean the part where I saved you from yourself?"

"You controlling, overbearing, arrogant son of a bitch! You think you own the world! You think you can tell me what to do and -- "

"I see Drew hasn't changed a bit," says a familiar voice. Mark Paulson's here, to our right, his face in profile, blond hair a lot longer than the last time I saw him. I catch his eye and see his eyebrows are arched, filled with questions.

"You got here fast," I snap at him.

He shrugs. "No traffic this time of night."

Lindsay's yelling continues unabated. " -- think you can kiss me and, and, take me to bed and that will change anything-- "

"This is *not* quite the Drew I know," Paulson says, turning away and coughing into his hand.

SLAP!

Distracted by Mark, I've given Lindsay her chance. She took it. My face absorbs the impact, which wasn't much. She has strong arms but bad aim. I can tell this is the first time she's ever slapped anyone.

I would laugh if I weren't rubbing my mouth, tasting a little blood.

And dealing with a shit-eating grin from Paulson, who gives me a look that says, *Better you than me, man.*

CHAPTER THREE

"Would you excuse us for a moment?" I ask, as if Mark had interrupted us at afternoon tea, and not in a moment of rage and humiliation and gun theft.

He turns away and heads toward a dark figure a hundred feet away. Must be Gentian.

I reach for Lindsay but she steps back, knees unlocked, thighs tight in a stance I recognize. It's from mixed martial arts and her fists are curled. She thinks she's going to fight me?

Cute.

Cute and *hot.*

"Lindsay, I'm Special Ops trained. You couldn't take me if you cloned yourself five times."

"I don't need to fight you and win, Drew. I just need to cause a little damage."

Oh, you already did, baby.

My chest squeezes, just enough to make me ache.

Can't say that out loud, though.

"I am trying to help you," I say slowly. Moonlight highlights the still-fresh scratches on her face, the awful bruising from the car accident, and her cheeks are flushed, rosy and fresh. She looks so gorgeous and raw, injured and feisty right now. It's inappropriate and completely dangerous to think this way.

I don't care.

I need to get through to her.

My hands aren't enough. Brute strength isn't cutting it.

I guess I have to resort to *feelings.*

"Beating me is your idea of helping? Why am I not surprised?" she says, her bitter tone making me wince. On the inside only, of course. On the outside, my face is polished granite.

"You can't do this. Not alone."

"Do what?"

"Hunt down those guys and kill them."

Her mouth makes a silent *O*.

"I wasn't – I wouldn't -- "

"Don't lie. I was. *I* would."

Her eyelids peel back in shock.

"But not like this, Lindsay. You're not being logical. This is no plan. You need tactics and strategy to win a war when you've lost so many battles already."

Her jaw is hard as steel, tight like a drum, and she's glaring at me like she doesn't want to hear a damn word I say.

But she's listening.

That has to be enough.

"I am here," I say slowly, "for my own reasons."

She huffs softly. "Last night showed me a few of your reasons." Her eyes flit to my crotch.

"Not *that*."

"You didn't like that?"

"Lindsay," I groan, running my hand through my hair and trying not to fuck her right up against the wall of her house, under her open window. "I didn't fall asleep with you in my arms in your bed because I have some ulterior motive!"

Her cheeks go pink.

And I go cold.

"No," I hiss. "Tell me you didn't."

"Didn't *what*?"

"Fake it."

"Fake *what*?"

"Fake everything last night just so you could convince me you really care about me and maybe there's hope. Fake it so you could trick me and get your hands on my gun and escape."

Snake eyes. Lindsay's looking at me with narrowed slits, reluctant to tell any truths. I can't blame her, but I do. She's ruining everything. Whatever half-baked scheme she thinks is going to work may very well destroy my carefully crafted machine that is designed to perform the same function:

Revenge.

"Here." She tosses a phone at my face, crossing her arms over her chest, her mouth tight. "Read that."

Come play with us, the text says.

And then another one.

AGAIN

Then three texted pictures. Harry shaking hands with Blaine Maisri at a political event.

The second pic turns me into a tingling body of stone and ice. I skip it. I force myself to look at the third texted picture of Blaine kissy-facing the camera.

"Fuck," I curse. My eyes dart to meet hers. I hold up the phone, the glowing screen pointed at her. "This is why you ran? *This?*"

"Wouldn't you?"

"No, Lindsay, that's the entire damned point. No, I wouldn't, not if I had a highly trained, highly motivated nine-member security detail assigned to me. No, I fucking wouldn't run, because I would trust the men whose entire purpose in life is to protect me."

"BUT YOU DIDN'T!" She explodes like a hand grenade tossed right into the middle of all four chambers of my heart.

"I TOLD YOU WHAT HAPPENED!"

"And they still raped me, Drew," she says, her voice low and intense. "Nothing you tell me about that night changes the fact that they just turned me into a bucket of flesh holes for their pleasure."

Flesh holes makes my throat spasm. "Nothing they did to you was about pleasure. It was about control. Power. Evil."

"That's exactly why I need to run away."

Something in her eyes changes the air between us. What happened? What isn't she telling me?

"That's why you need to stay next to me at all times," I counter.

Her slow blink is the only answer she gives.

I'll take it. It's better than no.

"Drew, what is that picture of you about?" she asks. The question feels like the weight of four years crammed into a handful of words.

"I've never seen that picture before."

"That's not an answer."

"What do you think it's about, Lindsay?" If they shared that picture with her, what else did they show her?

My skin turns to cold plastic. My mouth goes dry. The world turns into nothing but dark shadows and cold winds.

"You're naked in that pic. And you have blood all over you." She's staring at the ground, then her eyes click up to meet mine. "And my scarf is in the picture. What...what did you really do that night? Whose blood is that?"

Someone bangs an enormous gong in my head.

She's really asking if that's *her* blood.

The truth is, I don't know.

"I can tell you what I know," I choke out. "I know I didn't hurt you that night. I know they drugged me. I know I would never, ever willingly participate in what they did to you."

Mark Paulson clears his throat. I can't see him. He's behind a bush. The other guys must be getting antsy. You don't order a high alert and leave them hanging. Relieved by the interruption, I leave Lindsay hanging.

I can only handle so much. I'm made of steel when it comes to protecting other people, but even I have weaknesses.

Not many.

But this topic is one of them.

"And I know damn well, Lindsay," I add, grabbing her arms, pulling her to me with a fierce possession. "I know damn well I'll never, ever let them hurt you again."

"How am I supposed to know that, Drew?" Her words are a mixture of fury and a whimper that says she wants to believe me. "I see a picture like that and *of course* I wonder."

Those assholes. I open my mouth to explain. Or to try.

"Drew?" Mark calls out.

Saved by the bell.

"Tell Gentian it's covered," I call out to him. "We got it. No need to tell Bosworth."

Lindsay's shoulders sag with relief. Her eyes cut over to both of us, and when she meets mine, she's fuming. Aching with confusion and pissed as hell, but she's panting.

Exertion? Arousal?

I can't tell the difference in her anymore.

I reel back.

I call out to Mark. "But we have a new situation. You, me, and Gentian inside in Lindsay's bedroom in ten minutes. Tell the team to go back to normal stations. Crisis over."

Paulson leaves, and just as he's around the corner, Lindsay tries to run for it. Again.

I pounce, flattening her in seconds, belly to belly, and this time, she's not getting away.

Before she can say a word, my mouth's on hers, my body blanketing her, hips grinding into her, my cock hard and ready. None of this makes sense.

Not one movement, not one kiss, *nothing*.

She pushes up against me, her energy and anger directed through her mouth, her hands, the way she grabs my ass. Her hands pin me to her body. This is her volition. *Her* will. Her need is clear.

But confusing as fuck.

"You don't know what you're doing right now, Lindsay," I tell her, my mouth against her ear, shoulder digging into the mulch beneath us, our heads up against the wall of the house. We're filthy and sweaty, my fingers smelling like her, the memory of her coming against my hand so fresh.

"I know what I'm doing," she pants, nipping my lip, her hands like snakes, all over me, angry and feral, filled with a desperate hate that only passion can inspire.

"I would take you right here, up against the wall of your parents' house in the middle of the goddamn night like a rutting animal if you weren't...if I weren't -- " Words fail me. That happens more and more with her. I punch the wall with my free hand, my bones jarring with the impact, but at least it takes attention away from my pounding cock.

"If you weren't a coward?" Her chin juts up in that crazy way she has and that's it.

I go fucking *primal*.

Her fingernails dig into my shoulders, one hand threaded in my hair, her mouth is hot and heavy on mine, taking as much as I am, our lips bruising, tongues tangling in a ball of fury and lust. My hips push her into the ground as if I could pin her in place and make her stay there forever, to keep her from fleeing, my hard cock seeking her warmth, her breasts pushed against my chest with a soft, yielding feeling that is paradoxical compared to the wildcat trying to maul me alive with tongue and fingers.

"I hate you," she gasps against my mouth, but she kisses me again, sucking on my tongue, her hand wiggling between us to stroke me from the outside of my pants, my vision turning into storm clouds that billow and mushroom. My pulse sprints through my body like an Olympic runner going for gold and I can feel her getting close as I bend down and free myself, ready to lift her leg and slip inside her, give her what her dirty, naughty, rebellious little body needs.

The same body that left me in bed and stole my gun.

"Do it," she hisses. "Take me. C'mon, Drew. What are you afraid of? I want it. I want you. Let's just get it over with," she says, egging me on. Lindsay is an emotional pendulum. The arc is too wide.

Too extreme.

I chill immediately.

What the fuck is this game?

"No," I say, my voice ragged and torn, like she's shredded my vocal cords. "No way. I'm not going to screw you against the side of a building because you want to get it over with, Lindsay. I can't be some weird version of a revenge fuck."

My cock is screaming ten thousand different versions of *Yes, you can!* while the rest of me wants to duct tape her mouth shut and stick her on a helicopter back to that mental hospital because maybe Lindsay isn't done cooking yet.

She might need some more time there.

And I may be the biggest goddamned sucker on the planet.

"It's just sex, Drew," she says viciously, her hair a disaster, eyes practically glowing. I tuck myself back in, using every stress-control technique I can think of to regain impulse control.

I get in her face, our lips a half inch from each other, and my eyes cross until I can't see her anymore. All I see is red. "I am not going to let you turn me into a monster like those guys four years ago, Lindsay. I don't play that game. You can stand there and tell me you hate me after spending tender time in bed with me and letting me inside you just enough to know all of this is a big sack of shit."

Her lips curls up in a snarl, but I can see she's fighting on the inside. Lindsay's a great liar, but not when it comes to how she feels about me.

"Tell me the truth about that night," she insists.

"I already did." Except she's right – I didn't. I continue. "I won't help you in your quest to convince yourself that I am bad. I refuse. The first time we make love, it won't be in anger, and it sure as hell won't be up against the side of your house within earshot of a security detail you just emasculated."

She laughs. It's the sound of broken glass dropped on a tin roof. "*Who* did I emasculate, Drew?"

"You're not like this," I snap back, but the crazy fire in me is calming down. It has parameters now. Borders. I can manage this. I can get myself back to baseline.

"Like what?"

"Self-destructive."

"You think this is self-destructive? Hah! It's self-preservation!"

"The fact that you can't tell the difference makes you dangerous, Lindsay."

"Fuck you!"

"No. We've established that already. Quit begging."

"You *wish* I begged!"

Tension radiates like live wires between us. She's looking at me with such a mix of hatred, lust, and determination that I want to let her run away.

With me right on her heels.

But I can't.

Because I have a job to do.

I look up at the open window. "I assume you can't scale walls?" I ask her.

She huffs.

"Then we need to go back in the house the normal way. Through an actual door." I reach for her arm to guide her. She wrenches it away. My fingertips burn with the feel of her.

That's all I'm getting for now.

I guess it's better than nothing.

A Harmless Little Ruse

At least she's still here, weaving her way through the bushes alongside the house's foundation, finding grass and a stone path that winds around to the back door.

My gun is in my waistband. Lindsay's in sight.

Just another night at work, right?

CHAPTER FOUR

Lindsay sits on her bed, pretending to read on her phone. Her long blond hair is pulled back in a ponytail, eyes hard, mouth tight.

She looks like her mother.

The whole pretending-to-be-bored schtick makes her seem even more like Monica.

Except Monica really *is* bored most of the time.

Every few seconds, Lindsay's tongue pokes out to lick the tiny split in her lip. It's healing slowly from the car accident. God, that was just a few days ago, wasn't it? Time telescoped the second the helicopter landed on that island five days ago, when I checked her out and brought her back to her real life.

Paulson's standing near the door, taking it all in, silent. Gentian's nervous, primed for emergency where one no longer exists.

This is my tactical team. *This.*

I couldn't ask for better people.

"Is this going to take long? I'm hungry," Lindsay whines.

I roll my eyes.

"Should have thought about that before you decided to skip out on us and nearly create an international scandal."

"I aim to please," she says with a smirk, not looking up from her screen.

It's all an act. She knows it, I know it, and Paulson definitely knows it. He frowns, giving me a look that asks, *Fill me in later?*

I nod.

"Lindsay's attackers have been texting her. Started during or right after the car was tampered with."

Paulson perks up. "You trace the texts?"

"Yes. The first batch came from a phone registered to Lindsay."

Gentian and Paulson give her hard looks.

She finally reacts, dropping her phone, palms up. "I didn't do it!"

They look to me to verify.

"I was with her during the entire time when she allegedly bought the phone that the texts are from. She couldn't have done it."

"Not even an online purchase? Or set up someone else to do it for her?" Paulson asks.

"Fuck you," Lindsay exclaims. "I'm right here in the room! You're talking about me like I'm not even here. Of course I didn't do it!"

Paulson's eyes dart to her. "It's nothing personal. The truth never is."

She snorts.

"It's possible," I concede.

"Drew!" Lindsay gasps, her voice small and hurt. I wish she'd just yell at me. Now I feel like shit for hurting her. I am too reactive, too pumped.

Too emotional.

"But highly improbable," I continue. "She does know how to use the darknet, though. Could hire someone to do all this for her," I add. "Plus, she's using covert systems to communicate with her hacker. Book reviews written in code. Signing up for text message alerts for sweepstakes."

"Really simple tools," Mark muses.

Her eyes bulge. "How do you know I....?" She winces.

Ha. *Caught.*

"I suspected. We have evidence. You just confirmed it."

"I confirmed nothing other than the fact that I hate you."

I sigh.

Paulson smirks.

"I know." I give her a tight smile. "You've said that already, so no need to repeat yourself, sweetheart."

"But I never hired anyone to do this! I swear to God I'm not pretending to be in danger." The desperation in her voice makes my gut tighten. Her anger turns into a tearful plea to be believed.

I reach for her and press my palm on her shoulder. She closes her eyes, one tear trickling down the line of her straight nose, down the side of the nostril and over the crest of her upper lip. She's sending more mixed signals than a malfunctioning Super-8 ball.

"I know," I say softly. My emotions are all over the place.

Her eyes fly open. We look at each other, each second more intense than the last, until she's all that I see. All that I know.

All that I love.

And all that I protect.

"I know you didn't set this up. They did. They're gunning for you, and we need to figure out why."

"And stop them dead," Paulson adds.

Lindsay jolts. It's like she forgot other people were in the room, too.

"Dead?"

Paulson shrugs. "If that's what it takes."

"Oh," she whispers. Then her lips settle into a not-quite-smile that makes me hold my breath.

This would be so much easier if we could take John, Blaine and Stellan out, but that's not how this is going to work.

Nothing's simple when it comes to those three.

"You know where they are?"

"Yes."

"How'd they buy the phone under Lindsay's name?"

"Our darknet guy says they've been all over Russian sites and other places, hiring people to surveil her. Mimic her. It's four years ago, only with higher stakes."

"What do you mean?" Lindsay drops her phone and sits up, leaning intently, listening fully.

"We know *you* know this, Lindsay. Drop the act."

"Know what?" Her face is blank. Too blank. I know when she's hiding something.

"You have a friend who helped you access the darknet from your time on the Island."

Her eyes flicker with emotion she snuffs out, fast.

She says nothing.

"You've been communicating with him – or her – by using online retailer reviews."

She snorts. "You're crazy. Quit saying that."

"But I'm not wrong."

Paulson's eyes ping between us. He already knows this information. I told him earlier, when I figured it out and brought him in on the case.

"Do you have any idea how ludicrous you sound? Reviews? I'm using *book reviews* to communicate with someone? I'm not that nerdy."

"Let's pull up some of the reviews you've left on books lately, Lindsay. Shall we?" I pull out my own phone and tap the links I've stored in it.

Emotion fills her face.

It's anger.

"I don't have time for this crap, Drew. I'm exhausted, and Daddy's going to chew you out for wasting his time."

I ignore her and talk to Paulson instead.

"Clever, like I told you. If you're constantly being monitored, how do you communicate with someone your watchers aren't supposed to know even exists? You use code, right? Encrypted code. Except Lindsay isn't a developer. Not a coderchick. So what does she do? She uses books."

"Shut up, Drew."

"Reading's therapeutic, right?" I continue, ignoring her. "The people at the mental institution likely encouraged her to read. Pre-approved books. And when she asked for permission to leave reviews on book retailers, she probably got an enthusiastic *yes*. Her interest in literary pursuits was progress."

I flash her a look designed to put her on guard. "You picked some of the most ridiculous books, but you and your helper were smart. Self-help books. Make the staff think you were focused on self-care."

"You're inventing all this, Drew."

I smile. "I have your file from the Island, Lindsay. It's all in there." I know – and she knows – that I don't have all the information. That's okay.

Eventually I will.

Right now, though, I have to make her think I know more than I really do.

It's the only way to mine her for new information.

"You want me to think that." But she's shaky. She might as well give it up. I figured it all out two days ago.

Almost all of it.

Every bit except for the identity of her internet helper, but that'll come in time.

"*Finding Your Inner Bitch: 365 Ways to Be Angry*," I quote with a chuckle. Paulson smothers a grin. "Nice book. We decoded your review."

Lindsay just shakes her head slowly. She's fighting a grin, though.

"Want to know what it actually says? You used one of the simplest codes in the world. The third letter after each punctuation mark in the review is the message."

Lindsay's face twists into a mask of anger and she snaps, "Cipher."

"Excuse me?"

"If you're going to talk about how I communicated with him, have the intelligence to use the correct words. It wasn't a code. It was a cipher, dumbass."

We've progressed to name-calling. Great.

"She's got you there," Paulson mutters.

"I wasn't in this branch of military intelligence," I bite off.

"Biggest oxymoron ever," she says with a sigh.

"You pulled that old joke out? Oh, my hurt heart," I say, hand over my chest. "Bottom line: we figured it out. We know what you asked your contact to research, and we know you've been surveilling Stellan, Blaine and John for the last few months."

"Not surveilling. Just wanted to know where they were."

"But you acted like you didn't know about their success."

"I didn't! I only knew where they were. Not who they'd become."

"You're lying."

"I swear!"

"You've sworn before."

"But I mean it now!" She frowns. "I knew they were in the press. The first year there, I got secret Internet access. But the last two years they completely cut me off. That's why I started doing the book review things."

I give her an *I told you so* look.

"Fine. Yes, you figured it out." She half smiles. "I fooled everyone but you, Drew."

"Remember that, sweets. I will always know your secrets, especially if having them puts you in danger."

"Don't call me sweets! And I was never in danger. At least, not on the Island."

"What do you know about your internet informant?"

"Plenty."

"Who is it?"

She goes silent. Then she smirks. "You don't know, do you?"

Paulson cuts me a look. I'm pretty damn sure Lindsay doesn't know who her informant was, either. This whole situation stinks to high heaven. When you don't know who to trust, trust no one.

Fox Mulder had it right.

"No, I don't." Why not be honest? One of us has to be.

"Don't expect me to tell you," she says with a huff.

"I don't. Because you don't know, either."

She recoils slightly.

"We'll figure it out. Everyone leaves breadcrumbs."

"This isn't exactly Hansel and Gretel."

"It's pretty damn close, Lindsay."

Paulson looks at us both. "You need me, still?" The first rays of morning light peek through the window. I yawn. Jesus – it's got to be morning soon. A seven a.m. meeting for the day shift is coming on us fast.

"You want to come to the seven a.m. briefing?"

He glances at his phone. "Might as well. It's in forty minutes." He looks at Lindsay, then me, eyebrows up. "How about I go talk to the other guys and meet you in the conference room. Same place as before?"

I nod. He leaves.

"Aren't you leaving, too?" Lindsay's voice is hostile as hell, but two can play that game.

"Not yet."

Her long, heavy sigh should enrage me.

I laugh instead.

"You just put your life in danger. You put your father in danger by extension. And you're sitting here rolling your eyes and sighing like a tween with an attitude."

"You mean I put Daddy's presidential campaign in jeopardy."

"No. I said what I meant, Lindsay." I get right in her face. "You put his life in jeopardy. Because if you're kidnapped, do you have any idea what kind of bounty your kidnappers could demand? A presidential candidate's daughter?"

"He hasn't declared yet."

"You think that protects you? He's declaring tomorrow! You're on a plane tonight for Sacramento!"

"WHAT?"

Oh, shit. No one told her.

"Anya was supposed to brief you."

"Been a little busy, if you hadn't noticed."

Busy stealing *my weapon*.

Along with my heart.

"Considering I've been with you for ninety-eight percent of the time since you've been home, Lindsay, how could I *not* notice?"

"And yet you haven't." Hurt shines in her eyes as she looks at me. "Tomorrow? The official announcement's *tomorrow*?"

"He waited until you were home. We've kept the car crash out of the papers so far, but he wants to declare. And you have to be on stage."

"I don't have to do shit."

She's all bark and no bite. She'll go.

She has no real choice. All the rules are different when you're born into money and power.

If she refuses, Monica and Harry will put the thumbscrews on her. I should know.

They've gone over this contingency plan.

They'll call Stacia from the Island and turn her into Lindsay's on-site, 24/7 therapist. Therapeutic babysitter. If Lindsay thinks it's bad having my security detail on her like ants in a sugar bowl, wait until she sees the back up plan.

She's watching me as I think it through, waiting her out.

"They – those bastards can't get me. Not again."

"They won't."

"You keep saying that."

"Because it's true. Do what I tell you. Do what Harry asks. Just stick with the plan and don't deviate and we can get through this."

"The campaign?"

"No. That's a cakewalk, Lindsay. I'm talking about them." I gesture toward her phone. "Whatever game Stellan, Blaine and John are up to, they won't win."

"I hate this. I fucking hate this. I hate being under a microscope. I hate that I don't have my life. I hate being an extension of Daddy and being paraded around like a prized animal. I hate that I can't even flee my own awful life! I can't run away. Please, Drew, let me run away. Let me go." She dissolves into thick tears, her voice earnest and pleading.

It's the first sign of true emotion I've seen in her. Authentic. Raw.

And it breaks my heart.

But I can't say *yes*.

I can't.

Bending down, I don't touch her, but I do move closer. Her head's down and her hair's a mess, smashed with twigs and mulch, making her seem wild, feral, like a child of the forest, primeval and savage.

"I wish I could give you a better answer, Lindsay. But if you leave, you're a target. You'd be captured and used as a weapon against your dad."

"I'm a prisoner no matter what. I don't know who to trust."

I open my mouth to argue, then snap it shut.

She's right.

The truth hits me like she sucker-punched me.

She's one hundred percent right.

And that?

That I can't fix.

In fact, I'm one of her jailers.

"Jesus," I say softly, under my breath. "You're right."

She looks up sharply. "Huh?"

"You're right." The room spins. I'm still in control, but it takes effort. "You *are* damned if you do, damned if you don't."

She just blinks, over and over, as if in a trance. "You're...agreeing with me?"

"Yes."

Her eyes narrow. "Is this a trap?"

I sit on the ground next to her, my gun belt digging into my hip. It's a taunting reminder of the past hours. "No."

"No one ever agrees with me."

"I am."

"Then do something to help me."

"I *am*."

She huffs.

"But I'm also hurting you, and I'm so sorry for that."

She inhales sharply. "I have no idea what to say to that."

"Promise me you won't run away again, okay? Okay, Lindsay?" My turn to plead. "You promise me that, and I'll promise you this: I'll help you leave."

"What?"

It's the way she says that single syllable that breaks me. It snaps me in half. The word comes out as a tiny gasp of disbelief, a plea, a prayer.

"I mean it," I say, my voice thick with emotion. I can hear the change between us as much as I feel it. Nothing we're saying erases my fury about what she did to me or fixes her trust issues, but my perspective has shifted in just these handful of minutes.

I never thought I was part of the problem.

I always assumed I was part of the *solution*.

Harry and Monica want Lindsay to turn back time and be the good little girl she was four years ago. And if she can't comply, they'll bend her like a pipe cleaner and make her into a facsimile of what she once was, just long enough for the cameras to record the perfect family.

The American Dream.

Whether Lindsay wants that or not.

I can't stop them.

But I can't let her run away.

33

A Harmless Little Ruse

Which means I have to rethink everything I thought I knew.

As the first few sunbeams turn to a blinding shard of light, I look at Lindsay.

She's staring out the window, her eyes washed out by the sun, making them transparent.

They're the only part of her that is.

Chapter Five

"**M**ake-up! We need more under-eye concealer here! What on earth did you do last night, Lindsay – stay up for thirty-six hours while smearing charcoal under your eyes?"

Close.

Monica is her bright, cheery self as we get ready for the press conference in Sacramento, California's capital, where Senator Harwell Bosworth will declare his candidacy to run in the primaries for President of the United States.

Lindsay looks about as excited as wet toilet paper.

"Sorry, Mom," she says, but she doesn't mean it.

Paulson, Gentian, and twelve other guys on my team are here with me. All but Paulson and Gentian are assigned to watch Monica and Lindsay. We've expanded our role.

Harry's got his own separate team.

Mark, Silas and I have a specific target: we're watching for any hint of people going after Lindsay. The extra team within a team.

She hasn't had any new texts from those assholes. Harry's been briefed on the fingerprint issue with Lindsay's brake lines. It took a while to explain how someone could set her up like that, but Harry quickly absorbed the information.

And now here we are.

Showtime.

"Senator Bosworth," Paulson says, nodding to Harry, who stops cold in his tracks. His face splits with an incredulous grin.

"Thornberg! You're Thornberg's grandson. You have a different last name, though. Paul?" Given that Harry's known for remembering faces, this is a bit of a surprise.

"Mark Paulson, sir."

"Agent Paulson!" Harry snaps his fingers and shakes Mark's hand vigorously. "You made one hell of a bust with the El Brujo cartel." He pulls Mark in and says quietly, "Really helped me with this campaign, that whole mess. Having him wiped out boosted confidence in law enforcement and my numbers rode the coattails. Thank you for that."

Mark nods exactly once. He hates praise.

"What do they have you working on now, Paulson?"

"He's working for me," I say, interrupting.

The senator gives us both a half grin. "Good work. You're done with the DEA?"

Paulson shrugs. "A little time in the private sector never hurt anyone."

"You'd be a good contender in politics, Paulson. California will have an empty senate seat in two years."

"Yes, it will," Monica says smoothly, appearing at Harry's elbow. She's gorgeous, sophisticated and cool in the perfect ice-queen way that First Ladies need to possess, with a switch she can flip to be more down to earth. "And James Thornberg's grandson would come with built-in political capital." She takes in Paulson with an evaluative quality I don't like.

Don't like it one bit.

"Agent Paulson -- "

"Please. Just Mark, Mrs. Bosworth."

"If it's 'just Mark,' then it's 'just Monica,'" she jokes, flipping her hair off her shoulder. I can't tell if she's flirting, or worse.

"Have you met our daughter, Lindsay?"

Worse.

Lindsay stands up from her makeup chair, white bib around her neck, and grins at Mark with the eyes of an evil clown forced to pretend to be normal.

"Agent Paulson. We met yesterday." She shakes his hand.

Mark wisely says nothing, barely smiling.

Her hair person combs out the long blond strands, using a fat curling iron here and there to shape her style. Years ago, Lindsay told me all about the beauty rituals that were used for public appearances. The different makeup for studio shows.

Yet another kind of makeup for large stage appearances. How weather could ruin photo opportunities.

And how Monica insisted that Lindsay present herself as a perfect vision of the sweet, American Pie senator's daughter.

"We need to finish in here, Ms. Bosworth," the makeup person says, leading her back to the chair.

The senator peels Paulson and me off into a small huddle.

"Look, you two. I know there was a commotion at The Grove last night, and I don't have time for specifics. Your morning report was terse and vague," he says to me in an accusatory voice.

"But accurate."

I get a sour face in return. "That'll do for now, Drew, but after this announcement and the resulting flurry dies down, I need a full, off-the-record report." He glances around. "I want all the info you aren't even cleared to give Lindsay's handlers."

I nod. "Understood."

"And if you brought Agent Paulson in on Lindsay's security detail, it's clear there's more than meets the eye. I need to be in the know."

"And Mrs. Bosworth?"

"She's on a need-to-know basis." He smirks. "Monica's job is to keep up appearances. Leave the depth to me."

He leaves. Paulson shakes his head slowly. "Different senator, same behavior."

"What do you mean?"

"My grandfather was the same way."

"He ever run for president?"

"Nope. Said there was more power in the Senate. 'The Oval Office is a costume' was his standard phrase for politics and becoming president."

"Harry Bosworth clearly thinks otherwise," I reply.

"Good thing he does. Keeps you in billable hours for your security teams."

I snort. "This is babysitting."

"Babysitting with guns and snipers."

"Still just babysitting." I can't help but glance at Lindsay, who has her eyes closed as hair and makeup people do her eyeshadow and finish her up.

High-stakes babysitting.

"Show time!" Anya announces. She's dressed in a sedate grey suit designed to make her blend in. Monica's wearing a tasteful cream-colored suit with a black border at the lapels, mid-heel black shoes designed for climbing stairs without accident, and her hair and face are perfect.

First Lady material.

Lindsay's in a lovely dress with blue, red, black and cream, designed to coordinate with Harry and his red and blue tie, but not to outshine her mother. Everyone's smiling and waving. As the senator's arm goes up, all I can think about is a crazed gunman hitting the armpit.

Hey. It happened in 1981 with Reagan.

The potential for danger is everywhere.

Guns aren't my biggest worry here, though.

Lindsay is.

"Stage left you'll enter, with Mrs. Bosworth on the senator's left, and the daughter on the right."

Lindsay bristles at "the daughter." She recovers fast, though.

She's used to it.

Gentian and Paulson take their places at Stage Right and Stage Left. We're indoors, thank God, which means my team has less to worry about. Secret Service already swept the building, and private security is checking bags and clearing visitors. We could have a rogue element here, but chances are small.

Other than Stellan, Blaine and John, that is.

I've got every text coming in on Lindsay's phone echoing over to mine, so if they try that shit again, I'll be on it instantly. All my guys know they're working on Lindsay and Monica. Harry's covered by the Secret Service.

As long as each person does their job, stays in their zone, and doesn't turn into a cowboy, we're good today.

I'll deal with the unpredictable triad later.

I walk next to Paulson, steering clear of Lindsay, knowing my presence will just add to the massive case of nerves she clearly has. If appearances were all it took to play the part of picturesque future First Daughter, Lindsay would win the election for her dad.

Not that easy, though.

"Still no clear sense of what they're up to with those texts?" Paulson asks out of the corner of his mouth. Earbud in, full boring suit, and more weapons under his jacket than a prepper on Halloween night, Paulson's scanning the crowd while he talks to me.

"No. But they'll be subtle. These guys aren't going to shoot up a crowded theater."

"You have a way of helping me relax, Foster."

"Doing my job."

"Yes, boss."

Strange words coming from my commanding officer on my first tour in Afghanistan.

"Care to explain the picture with you in it?"

"Already did."

"I think there's way more to it than you're telling."

I don't say a word.

We give each other dry looks and I move on, watching the scene intently.

"...a man who needs no introduction, Senator Harwell Bosworth!"

The public address system crackles with the roar of the crowd, thousands of people applauding, stage lights blinding but necessary. I look across the dark back of the stage and see Lindsay standing next to Gentian, blinking furiously, her face a slab of granite.

No emotion.

You'd never have guessed what happened yesterday ever occurred. We're all professionals. We are about action, not emotion. Control, not impulse. Every calculated move is designed to support the man on stage right now, the guy with both arms in the air waving, and that's when it hits me.

I've been hired to control.

To control Lindsay.

To keep her in a state of agitation and worry.

If I weren't here, in charge of her, she wouldn't be constantly – *viscerally* – reminded of my role in the massive clusterfuck of four years ago.

The senator and Monica want her to be uncertain. They want her to be unsteady. If she were centered and grounded, she'd be powerful.

A force.

Demanding.

And the last thing a man who's leveraging his way up the ladder to become the leader of the free world wants is a daughter with a sense of her own true strength.

The blood drains out of my face as I watch Lindsay touch Gentian's arm, stand on tiptoes, and try to get him to step out of his role and smile at her.

He's steady as a Beefeater.

Good man.

All across the country, over the next few months, similar stage displays will happen. Republicans and Democrats and Libertarians and Independents and Greens and smaller political parties will have people declare their candidacies for the primary runoffs, to become the party candidate in the actual national election in November, two years from now.

Harwell Bosworth isn't all that special.

He's been in politics for most of Lindsay's life, but he's at the beginning of the long slog to the White House. So are all his rivals, each competing for the top spot.

A position people would kill to have.

How far would you go to be leader of the free world?

"Drew?" It's the dispatcher at my call center. "Ready for a transmission?"

"Bad timing."

"You said if anything came in from that number -- "

"Scarves?" That's our code for Stellan, John and Blaine.

"Yes."

"Go."

"New text." I watch in slo-mo as Lindsay reaches into her purse to retrieve her phone.

"What's it say?"

"*'What color is your underwear?'*"

"Not funny!" I shout, exploding.

"That's what the text says, sir!"

"Fuck."

MELI RAÎNE

"And a new one says, '*We can't wait to find out. And we will.*'"

I tear off stage, knowing I can't bullet my way across in view of the crowd, needing to get to Lindsay before she reads that fucking text. They're toying with her, mindfucking her before the biggest performance she's faced in four years, and I don't care how much she's hurt me in the last two days, or how angry I am at her for stealing my gun and lying to me, she's still a human being.

And my client.

And I still love her.

"Gentian," I snap into my headpiece. "Don't let her read her phone. Repeat – don't let Lindsay read her phone."

"Yes, sir."

I can't see anything, can only thread my way through the overcrowded backstage area and hope Harry drones on and on in his speech about how wonderful America is and he buys me enough time. Gentian can take the emotional hit of having Lindsay get pissed at him.

But if she reads those texts...

"I'm not allowed to have a phone anymore? What are you talking about, Silas?" Her voice is high and hysterical, at a pitch that says she's beyond irritated, anxiety in full force.

"He's following orders," I say, gasping, winded not by the effort of getting here but by the sheer power of the mess unfolding before me.

"Why?"

"You don't want to read what's on your phone."

Alarm fills those gorgeous brown eyes and she stands, frozen, like she's made of wax. Monica's watching us from her side of the stage, shaking her head, mouth a firm line of carefully painted lipliner. Her anger is justified.

So is Lindsay's terror.

"They texted me again?" Lindsay gasps.

Can't lie to her.

"Yes."

"Are they *here*?"

"They can't hurt you."

"That's not an answer!" Her voice is shrill, like an air raid siren.

41

"I don't know. But we have you covered."

"Covered?"

"Lindsay." I reach for her elbows, cradling her trembling bones in my hands. "They. Are. Not. Going. To. Get. You."

"...and I couldn't be the effective senator without my lovely, extraordinary wife, Monica Bosworth!" Harry's arm sweeps toward Monica in that exact moment. The crowd goes nuts, cheering, as Monica moves with catlike grace across the stage, into Harry's arms for a carefully rehearsed cheek kiss, followed by a kiss on the lips. Not too racy, but not stodgy.

Just right for national television clips.

"I can't do this, Drew." Lindsay's knees go weak and my hold on her tightens. "I thought I could, but I can't."

"You can. You will. It's one hug with both your parents, ten minutes of standing there with a smile on your face, an arm reach in the air holding hands, and some waving. You can do that."

"Not with those bastards stalking me."

"They're stalking you whether you're on stage or not. On stage, I can watch you carefully. My team knows about the text by now. We're all on heightened alert."

She starts breathing again. I didn't realize she'd been holding her breath.

"Can't turn back now. Your dad and mom will gesture to you any minute."

Her face goes blank.

One long, deep breath. Two. Three. Lindsay transforms before my eyes. She's still shaking, but now her face gets some color in it again, cheeks pink. She flashes a fake smile at me.

With dead eyes.

"You're right. This is show time. I've spent four years hiding from the world – against my will – and now it's time to prove to Mom and Daddy that they were wrong."

"Exactly!" Pride fills me, making it hard not to touch her right now. Public appearances have to be maintained, though.

"And when this is over, you're helping me to escape."

"Huh?"

"You said so." Triumph fills her voice.

"...daughter, Lindsay!" Harry's giving us a smile that looks so sincere, but under those friendly eyes he's saying, *Get your ass on stage.*

Lindsay peels away from me and walks with great confidence into her father's arms, fluid as a gazelle, graceful and confident. The crowd claps politely, a few catcalls and hollers a bit much.

A quick kiss on Monica's cheeks and the two women wrap their arms around each other's waists, staring adoringly at Senator Bosworth, who begins the true speech of the night.

"I stand before you tonight as a proud Californian and a United States senator..."

My attention stays on Lindsay at all times, body tense yet loose, ready to jump into action whenever needed. Paulson and Gentian are scanning the crowd. My team knows what Stellan, John and Blaine look like, but there's no way they'd actually be here. They wouldn't do their own dirty work. Not now. Too much to lose.

Whoever they send to try to hurt Lindsay is going to be an unknown. And I suspect they won't be so blatant. Not their style. This cat-and-mouse texting game is more their speed. In the fight between the mindfuck and overt physical violence, they'll take the mindfuck every time.

Harry stands on stage looking and sounding presidential. Only the security team can look at Lindsay and see what's wrong. Her body's angled just so against her mother, leaning for support. Monica's shouldering it, but her eyes reflect a level of irritation Lindsay will pay for later.

Attagirl.

Get through this. You can do it.

As Harry's voice takes on the stronger, firmer tone that comes with whipping the crowd into a rhetorical frenzy, I see Lindsay relax. This is the downhill. Like riding a bike up a killer mountain, Lindsay is aching, screaming for relief, and now she's crested, the rest of the speech smooth sailing. I see her move an inch away from Monica, her shoulders squared, her body language morphing.

I got this, her body says.

I got it.

A Harmless Little Ruse

"When I am your president, I will..." Harry's refrain generates shockwaves from the crowd, my earpiece exploding with noise, men reporting in to announce suspicious backpacks, people hovering at entrances, and the small accumulation of oddities that come with public events. None of them are noteworthy, nothing that rises to the level where I need to intervene.

Dotted throughout the crowd are supporters with clusters of balloons, red white and blue for the colors of the American flag. Balloon bunches rise up from the legs of the crowd in what is clearly a coordinated effort. It gives the stadium a whimsical look.

Harry makes a final statement, then two staffers walk on stage to hand Monica and Lindsay respective bunches of flowers.

Lindsay begins to sway on stage as she's handed her bundle. Something's off. Monica's fine, taking her batch of white roses dotted with blue and red carnations, but Lindsay is holding hers like it's a bunch of live snakes. The colors are different. Her smile fades, the panic in her eyes running down her face as she looks up above the crowd.

Out of the corner of my eye, I see a bunch of multi-colored balloons lifting, letting go and allowed to float above the masses. It's a group of three balloons.

The colors match the flowers in Lindsay's hands.

Blue.

Red.

Purple.

The same color as the scarves those bastards used to bind her four years ago.

CHAPTER SIX

Monica's smile doesn't even falter. Only her right eye twitches slightly as Lindsay stares at the bunch of flowers, head tipped down now, not looking out at the crowd with her agreed-upon performance smile.

And then the corners of Lindsay's mouth spread wide. I see it before she looks up, and as the stage lights catch her face in slow motion, she comes up grinning.

It's practically homicidal.

From a distance, though, you can't tell the difference between a super-exuberant, vibrant young woman and a woman who is ready to commit murder.

But *I* can.

Lindsay walks right past Monica, her eyes staring out at the thousands who cheer, confetti and balloons in the air now, the tri-colored balloon bunch lost into the cavernous ceiling of the auditorium.

She holds the bouquet of flowers high above her head. I follow her at the side of the stage and tell my guys at the edge of the front row to get ready.

The flowers launch as she throws them into the crowd, then looks right out at dead center, her palm pressed to her lips, throwing the crowd a big kiss.

Euphoric cacophony erupts.

And then she turns around and walks into the waiting arms of her father.

That was as close as Lindsay could get to giving Stellan, Blaine and John the middle finger in public.

"Track down the source of Lindsay's flowers and the red, blue and purple bunch of balloons in the crowd," I snap to Gentian.

"Yes, sir. Need lockdown?"

"No. Damn it, we can't risk the PR mess. Just get a fast handle on who was where. Review video. Front of stage, center, first row area is where I saw the balloons. Same area where Lindsay threw her bouquet."

I skate through the thick crowds behind stage, knowing I have to get back to Lindsay, wondering what I'll find.

"Drew?" It's Paulson.

"What?"

"Balloons held by a stoner. Said 'some dude' handed him a fifty to walk in and release the balloons."

"It's always 'some dude,'" I mutter.

"Wish I had better news."

"Cameras outside where the stoner met the culprit?"

"Probably not. Said it was two blocks away."

"Check anyway."

"Got it."

A wall of wavy blonde hair attached to the same dress Lindsay wore catches my eye. Monica is on the other side of her, eyebrows turned down, face otherwise hard as stone.

And just as expressive.

"What are you talking about, Lindsay? Colors?"

That's all I need to hear.

"Monica, the attackers are harassing Lindsay again. First cutting the brake line, then a series of harassing texts, and today they upped the ante." I whisper this into her ear, breathing in the heady scent of her spicy perfume, like cinnamon mixed with copper.

She jolts, then tenses. "No press leak?"

"None. We're careful."

Her shoulders relax. "Good. Maybe Harry didn't make a mistake hiring you, after all."

She walks away.

Lindsay's been watching our conversation with keen eyes. "I'm fine, Mom," she says in a falsetto voice. "Thanks for asking. No, no, don't shower me with so much concern."

It's a tough day for everyone. I start to say that, then stop myself.

Because it's hardest of all on Lindsay.

"Paulson's working on locating the people who provided the flowers and balloons," I say as we walk rapidly to the back doors where the SUV's waiting for us. I see Gentian with Monica, escorting her out to meet up with Harry for post-announcement press junkets.

We've been ordered to take Lindsay back to The Grove. She's not allowed to be interviewed.

Strict orders.

"Tonight was a success!" Lindsay says in a fake, breathy voice. "From the senator's perspective, the moment was a triumph. Lindsay didn't spew green soup, a sniper didn't pick off Harry, and Monica was having a perfect hair day."

"Lindsay."

"I wish I could drink myself into oblivion."

"Why don't you?"

"Because everything I'm trying to escape will still be here in the morning."

"Does that include me?"

She says nothing.

I regret the question instantly.

"Sir?" Gentian speaks into my earpiece. "Texts confirmed from a new phone purchased with Lindsay's credit card."

Damn it. "Same store?"

"No."

"Research any similarities between this purchase and the last one. We need to figure this out."

"Yes, sir."

A familiar dread tickles the back of my neck, dragging along my spine.

Inside job?

Is someone on Senator Bosworth's staff – or God help me, my own – doing this to Lindsay?

"Can you think of anyone on the household staff or your father's staff who would set you up like this?"

"Aside from you?"

"Not funny."

"Not kidding."

"You seriously think that I'm making it look like you cut your own brake line, bought the phones that are sending you threatening texts, and paid off some guy in the crowd to bring in colored balloons that matched your flower bouquet, all while being in charge of your private security?"

"It's not out of the realm of possibility."

"Jesus, Lindsay!" My pulse skyrockets. "If you really think any of that *is* within the realm of possibility, you need to talk to your father and mother. Have me taken off the case. I'll quit right now. You never have to see me again." It hurts to say that.

She jolts.

"Good riddance. Because I can't work with someone who suspects me of that level of mindfucking sabotage." *I can't be in love with one, either.*

She just shrugs.

"Gentian!" I snap into my mouthpiece. "You and Paulson are in charge. I'm out."

Fury turns my vision a cold white as I find the nearest Exit sign. Paulson appears to my right as Lindsay opens her mouth to say something.

I storm away, crashing through the metal double doors into the blinding sun, unable to think or feel. The world inside is nothing but fuzz. Outside, everything lives in stark, crisp clarity. Sound and touch and taste and wind and car exhaust and everything blends.

I walk and breathe. Walk and breathe. Curse and fume. Curse and fume until I'm in my black SUV and pull out my laptop.

"She fucking thinks I'm setting her up. She – *what*?" I mutter to myself, fingers flying on the keyboard as I open programs I hope the NSA doesn't know exist. The looming threat of Stellan, Blaine and John is like a thundercloud that builds and builds, twisting into a tornado high in the sky.

Filled with sharks.

I snort at the image. It's not funny. Nothing about any of this is funny. But we made it through the senator's announcement and all I know is that those assholes from our past are out there, playing a cat-and-mouse game that I need to control.

And fast.

Lindsay's little darknet contact has been feeding her information all along. She knew more than she let on. How deceptive has she been this whole time? Has she been playing the innocent while double-crossing me?

And why?

If you know the *why* in a given mystery, you can figure out the *how*.

Why would Lindsay keep all this knowledge under wraps? Why did she tap into someone using the darknet in the first place?

But more important:

Why is this person helping her?

And how reliable are they?

If she's trusted every scrap of information this person has fed her while they've worked together, then she could be in even more danger than I realized. Bet it never occurred to her that her contact could be a plant.

Someone Stellan, John and Blaine set up to screw with her.

Tap tap tap.

I look up to find Lindsay glaring at me through the tinted window, with Gentian behind her, rolling his eyes.

I ignore her.

"Drew!" she shouts. "Don't make me make a scene!"

There is a crowd of media behind her, cameras pointed at different angles so the talking heads can get their ninety-second clips. If she draws their attention by yelling more, this victory could quickly turn to defeat.

Setting the laptop aside, I snap the door open and grab her wrist, pulling her into my lap. Gentian closes the door quickly, turns around, and leans his back against the window.

Good man.

I can smell the anxiety pouring off her skin, her body stone cold and trembling at the same time, oddly still, yet buzzing. Her skirt hikes up and the thin triangle of cotton from her panties reveals itself between her thighs.

"What the hell are you doing?" she shouts. We're in the passenger seat, which is pushed all the way back, and she's wriggling, her long hair in my face.

I wrap my arms around her and tighten them. She can't leave.

I won't let her.

"You want to talk to me?" I say dryly.

"Not like this!"

"Talk."

"Let me go!"

"Let you go *where*?"

"I can sit in the driver's seat." But she's slowing down, settling into my lap. One heel from her shoe digs into my shin, but I don't care. She smells like fear and sugar.

Lindsay is the only woman who does this to me.

Drives me up a fucking wall and makes me want to hold her for eternity.

"Whatever you've been doing on the darknet needs to stop, Lindsay."

"Oh, God. Another lecture."

"It's my job. And you didn't deny it."

"Your job is to protect me. My mom's job is to lecture me. Are you my mom now?"

"If you have mistaken me for Monica, you have more serious issues than I'd ever imagined."

A reluctant snort comes out of her. She calms in my arms, then slumps her shoulders with a sigh. "Do I have to sit in your lap for this conversation?" She wriggles her ass against me. "It's getting uncomfortable." Her eyes meet mine and she smirks.

Damn it.

I run my hand along the lines of her arm, tight with muscle and a little too thin. She's dropped weight since she went to the Island. Four years changed her. She's gorgeous in every way possible, but the worry lines in her forehead make me want to steal her away. Remove her from this gigantic mess.

My job, though, is to keep her right in the middle of it all.

Keep her safe.

She moves out of my lap without words, her ass suddenly in my face as she crawls over the console to get into the driver's seat.

"Nice view."

"Shut up."

Her thighs slide against mine, her legs bare and tan, smooth as spun silk. Blood pounds through me, rushing with a massive tingle to every pore in my body. I tense. If she doesn't get her skin away from me in about two seconds, I'll end up kissing her in here.

And I can't do that.

I can't do that because it wouldn't be just one kiss.

And going at it with Lindsay in a tinted SUV limo in front of a hundred media outlets is the very definition of *not* doing my job.

Lifting one knee, she moves, her panties in my face. I close my eyes, thinking about baseball scores, Jabba the Hut, Monica – anything to get this raging hard on under control.

"Foster?" someone barks in my earpiece. "Paulson here. Gentian says you have Lindsay?"

"Yes."

"One of the scarves is present."

All the passion in my blood is instantly replaced with a cunning rage designed for battlefields.

"Copy. Track him. Anywhere near us?"

"No. But he's shaking hands with the senator."

"Fuck.

"Who is it?"

"Blaine Maisri. From what I overheard, he's here to congratulate the senator on his presidential run. They're talking about him making a run for Senator Bosworth's old House seat. Something about Nolan Corning helping with the campaign?"

"Copy." Nolan Corning? That's Harry's biggest rival in the party. It's widely believed Corning's going to run in the primary, too, against Harry. Why would Corning back *Blaine* of all people for Harry's old House seat?

I can't focus on the intrigue right now.

The SUV is tiny. If Lindsay has good ears, she heard most of that. Knows that Blaine is right here.

I look at her.

She meets me with eyes the size of saucers. "Blaine," she whispers, her voice filled with terror.

"Track him. I'll get Lindsay out of here."

"Will do."

"We need to trade places," I snap at Lindsay. She starts to open the door. I reach across her and grab her hand.

"Not like that, Lindsay. Cross over me."

"What?"

"I don't want you getting out of the car."

"Who is 'scarf'?"

"You don't need to know."

"It's a code name."

"Yes."

She frowns, then her entire face morphs into a mask of rage. "You call them all 'scarf'? Seriously? Whose sick idea was that for a code name?"

I ignore that. She doesn't need to know that her own mother came up with the name.

"Sir." It's Gentian. "Senator Bosworth wants you back in here."

"He what?"

"Wants you back in here. Now. He's talking with the scarf."

"Is he in danger?"

"No, sir."

I gave Lindsay a hard look. "Stay here."

"You can't make me."

"I'm not going to debate that. Let's just say I can." I climb out of the SUV before she has a chance to reply. Gentian's back is still pressed against the door.

"Keep her in there. I don't want her seeing any of the scarves." Hell, a part of me doesn't want to see Blaine, either.

Another part can't fucking wait.

"Yes, sir."

"Gentian, get a confirmation on all hallways or corners not covered by video camera."

"Jones already did, sir. The small alcove between the bathrooms and the loading dock has a tiny portion that isn't covered by the angle of either camera in that area. It's a dead zone of about six feet wide, right in front of a labor law sign."

"Got it."

I march back into the backstage area and my guys guide me, through glances and microgestures the average person wouldn't notice, until I take a deep breath before turning a corner, knowing what I'll see.

Harry, chatting with Blaine Maisri.

My mouth spreads into a smile that never, ever comes close to reaching my eyes.

"Drew! You remember Blaine, don't you?" I can't read Harry right now. He's looking at me, but I might as well be looking right back at a white wall. "He's an up-and-coming state representative who's making a play for my old House seat."

I nod curtly at Blaine, who gives me a smirk. "Maisri," is all I say. The less spoken, the better. The guy who gives as little as possible is the one who wins.

These scarves already took damn near everything from me four years ago.

They don't get another drop from me.

"Foster." His eyes don't even meet mine.

Lindsay keeps calling me a coward, but the real one is right here.

My grin widens. "Good to run into you."

His head jerks up and this time, I realize why he won't look at me.

He's fucking terrified.

Adrenaline shoots through me like a line of napalm set on fire.

"Actually, I was hoping to have a word with you," I say, pretending to be chummy, working my throat like it doesn't have an elephant in it.

The fear in his eyes disappears as if someone has programmed him, and his circuits have been rewired. His eyes light up as if he's excited. Stoked.

Eager.

"Really? For old times' sake?"

"Maisri has the backing of Nolan Corning," Harry explains, as if I don't know, his eyebrows going up with fake admiration. Those eyes are calculating, just like Lindsay's. "On the fast track. Twenty or thirty years from now, you could be in the White House," he says to Blaine, who doesn't even bother with false modesty.

"From your mouth to the voters' ears," Blaine answers with a grin.

A Harmless Little Ruse

A photographer snaps pictures. Harry grabs Blaine's hand and turns at an artful angle, controlling the picture. Image shaping is everything.

"You high school buddies go at it. I have more flesh to press," the senator says, clapping Blaine on the shoulder in that collegial way men in power have.

So do I.

With my knuckles.

"Tell Corning I said *hi*," Harry calls over his shoulder to Blaine.

A white rage I haven't felt since combat back in Afghanistan fills me. It's a hyper-energy, so strong I can barely control it, so addictive I want to feel it forever. Unnerving and maddening, it has a will of its own, taking over, hijacking me.

In combat, it's my greatest asset other than my weapon.

As a security specialist, it's like a nuclear bomb. A great deterrent if you don't actually unleash it into the world.

"What the hell do you have to say to me?" Blaine hisses. "We have nothing to talk about. Ever."

I nod toward the dead zone Gentian identified.

"Over here. Away from prying ears. Some things are better kept private, right?"

He makes a sour face. "I don't have time for this shit."

"You keep threatening Lindsay and you're a dead man," I say quietly, with a smile, as I reach for his shoulder and clap him on the back.

He looks like he's choking on a snake.

I know how this works. The video cameras don't have sound. If I'm careful, I can make it look like this is just a conversation between two old buddies, meeting by coincidence. The rising political star running into the owner of a private security company. The California state representative having a chat with the Purple Heart recipient.

The presidential candidate's decorated war hero security detail shooting the shit with his old friend.

At least, I have to make it look like that until I can get him out of camera range.

"You're threatening me?" He moves his shoulder away, then looks up, searching for a camera.

I grin. We're a handful of steps away from the labor law sign.

"I'm warning you." He hasn't denied the threat to Lindsay. My white rage turns red. Sonofabitch.

"It goes both ways."

"You can't prove a fucking thing."

A gong goes off in my head, like someone took the biggest felt-covered mallet in the world and rang the sun.

"You sick motherfucker," I growl. "You don't even deny it."

His turn to give me a distorted grin. "Why would I deny anything to you, Drew? You're next."

Three feet. We're three fucking feet from the dead zone when I hear --

"Drew? You can't just leave me in a hot car to bake and – " Her voice cracks, going subsonic. "Oh my God. Oh my God, no. You weren't kidding. No, no..."

We both turn, Blaine moving in slo-mo, my red rage making every part of the hallway look like I'm on a fast train through a city of lights, all the white flying past me in pinpricks turned to lines.

One step.

Two steps.

I pivot, inserting myself between Blaine and Lindsay, acting as the shield I could never be on that night four years ago.

I act.

I do.

I am.

I *will*.

"Lindsay," Blaine says, his voice low with pleasure, moving toward her.

The sound of her name coming out of his mouth breaks me.

My fist hits his face with a satisfying crunch as the fury drives me forward, like a spirit that inhabits my body and takes over. It feels good. Right. Powerful, my body going into overdrive as I do exactly what I need to do in this monumental moment. Four years.

Four years.

He moves back, his nose bloodied, eyes wild with some mix of confusion and outrage, his mouth opening to say something, but I fill those lips with my fist, turning this punch into my final blow, the one that has to be enough for four years ago.

And yet I have no logic, no rationality, no strategic purpose as my rat brain kicks in and does the job. The second punch makes my thumb joint slip between his teeth, saliva on my hand, the feel of the corner of his mouth tearing a brutal victory.

Lindsay's breath on my ear, her small hands pulling on my shoulders, snap me out of it.

"Drew! You're on camera!"

"You're the dead man now, Foster," Blaine hisses through a mouthful of blood. His eyes are unfocused. He's not looking up. If he looks at Lindsay, so much as glances her way, I'll crush his head with one targeted kick.

"Drew! Stop! You're going to be arrested. He's not worth it."

That makes Blaine look up.

"You sick piece of shit," she says. Her calf pulls back like she's about to kick him.

A swarm of people come running down the hallway to my back. I hear the footsteps. Lindsay jumps out of the way, runs to the loading dock door behind Blaine, and opens it. I have no idea what she's doing, and reach for her, wanting her behind me so I can protect her from Blaine, and then someone's got my arms snapped behind me in a locked grip.

"Representative! What happened?"

"Someone assaulted the representative!" Lindsay gasps, pointing to the now-open door. "He went that way!"

My arms drop instantly, but I feel the heat of the security guy behind me, waiting for orders from Blaine.

"She's ly -- " Blaine gives me a shrewd look, then glances at the ceiling. His eyes float behind my shoulder. "Review the video."

"There isn't any here, sir. We lost visual on you, then heard shouts."

Blaine looks at me in disgust, eyes narrowed.

"You're wasting time!" Lindsay shrieks, pointing. "I witnessed the whole thing! Drew was protecting Representative Maisri and tried to punch the attacker, but he fled. All three men were just a pile of people. I was on my way to the restroom and found them and started calling for help!" Her eyes float to the women's restroom two doors down.

Every second she calculates, every comment she makes, gives the story credence. Nice touch using his title.

My own guys appear, five of them, Gentian among them.

"Sir?" he asks, eyes cold, assessing the situation, knowing damn well what I just did.

"We need medical attention for Representative Maisri." I look at him. "I'm sorry for the accident. I was trying to hit the target."

Trying my damnedest.

Blaine gives me a rueful look as one of the members of his security detail hands him a handkerchief for the blood. Two medics appear, carrying a large first aid kit. "My team will investigate this."

"Of course," I say, nodding. Lindsay's behind me, gushing out lie after lie to a group of security guys who listen intently. She's got them wrapped around her little finger, spinning a story about events that never, ever happened.

Three of Blaine's security team are already out the door, chasing an assailant who doesn't exist.

"Oh, oh!" Lindsay says, grabbing Gentian's arm. He braces her. "I'm – it's so warm in here. I'm feeling faint," she says, her voice tinny and thin. She used to faint sometimes...before.

Four years ago. When I knew who she was.

I have never met this version of Lindsay before.

She's exciting as fuck and frighteningly calculating.

Gentian brings her to a seat. All the attention's on her now, as handlers bring water bottles, one of the paramedics checking her pulse. Our eyes meet and she says in a weak voice, "Just get the man Drew tried to take care of!" with an impassioned plea worthy of an Oscar. "We just want to see Representative Maisri get the justice he deserves." She lowers her head between her knees and sniffs.

Λ Harmless Little Ruse

"We're taking care of that threat, sir," I say nice and loud, so everyone can hear me.

Blaine just looks at me with eyes as hard as the barrel of my gun.

Chapter Seven

Hitting someone always involves paperwork.

Gentian takes Lindsay back to The Grove with extra security and instructions that only he, or Paulson, is her core person. I have to stay at the event to wrap up the police report on the "attack" and to manage all the final issues that arise from running a company and being in charge of protection for Monica and Lindsay.

By midnight, I'm at my apartment's security kiosk, the RFID chip on my car triggering the safety gate for the parking lot. Five minutes later, I'm nursing a swollen hand, a beer, and a renewed taste for blood.

I can't stop reviewing those few minutes, over and over. Blaine always struck me as the weakest of the three, the follower, the guy who went along to be part of the crowd. It's sickening, really.

Once I became an officer in charge of men like him, I realized they make great soldiers, but terrible strategists. Tell them what to do, stoke them up and make them think they're part of something great, that their identity as part of the group is more important than any moral code outside the group, and you're golden.

They're yours to do whatever you command.

And while that's great when your mission is good, when people like Blaine are controlled by someone whose sights are set on evil, these followers are the worst form of humanity. They're the foot soldiers in concentration camps, the ones "just following orders." They're the people who support the bullies at the bus stop when kids get beaten. They're the crowd of teasers on social media who encourage a kid to kill himself.

They are the tools of evil.

And without them, evil can't thrive.

But they outnumber the good two to one.

Blaine is a follower. A foot soldier. A smart but pliable guy who puts external approval above doing the right thing.

That makes him dangerous.

But not as dangerous as whoever pulls his puppet strings.

All this philosophizing is a convenient excuse to avoid thinking about my feelings for Lindsay. Sympathy for what she's going through. Passion for the minutes she was in my lap. Terror for the moments when those balloons and flowers came into the picture.

Arousal for the memory of her taste in my mouth.

Anger for the fact that she still doesn't trust me.

By my second beer, I'm loose enough to go take a shower, wash off the shit of the day, maybe start to clear my head. My apartment is basic, furnished mostly from leftover furniture from my parents' home. We sold it, my sister and I, after they died. Well, *she* sold it. I couldn't be here, too busy on combat missions, too crazed to come back home for more than the funeral.

The leather recliner dad loved is my favorite. I rented an apartment on the ocean, with a deck, and I plunk down into the chair, looking over the water through my open patio door. If I sit on the deck, the next-door neighbor will invite me over to share a pitcher of margaritas, and I don't want that.

You need to spend a lot of time alone when you do what I do for a living.

The alone time recharges my batteries. More than that, it helps make me fit for human company again.

You can't kill people in an effort to protect and not have it change your soul.

Sometimes, the soul needs beer and pizza to even think about recovering.

After a minute of ocean-staring time, I realize it's not working. Solace isn't helping. All I can think about is Lindsay. Being intimate with her. Talking and bantering with her. Protecting her.

Kissing her.

Am I crazy to think that we have a chance? I don't think so. There's no reason we can't overcome the wounds. The scars will always be there, a map that reminds us of the past, but we have room in our lives to make new memories. Forge new commitments. Create a stronger bond.

A perfect love between two imperfect people.

I know she wants me as much as I want her. I know she's scared and in reactive mode, wavering between fury and agreement.

Getting her to trust me is my actual mission, I see.

A wave crashes hard against the shore and I realize we're like the tides. An invisible force pulls us toward and away, close then far, the back and forth inevitable.

An ache in my bones, my biceps, my heart, my cock turns emotional and physical at the same time, making me vibrate for her. I can't do this. I can't not be with her.

I rub my face with my palms and wonder if I can get away with going back to The Grove to see her tonight. Under what pretense?

And will she care?

Tap tap tap.

I fly up, gun in hand, pointed at my front door, finger on the trigger. No one visits me. No one. Ever. I've trained the next-door neighbor not to knock on my door. She knows. If I'm on the deck, I'm fair game.

Otherwise, stay the hell away.

"Foster? It's Paulson."

Shit.

"What the fuck, Mark? You know to call first."

"I did. Went to voicemail."

"Something wrong with Lindsay?" My blood sends a plume of heat through me.

"She's fine."

The heat doesn't recede.

"Then why are you here?"

"Because you're *not* fine."

I groan.

"Can we talk without the fucking door between us? Don't you have any manners, Drew?"

I holster my weapon and sigh, looking at the half-empty pizza plate and remaining beers in the six-pack.

"Left them all in Afghanistan," I mutter as I unlock the door and open it to find Mr. Blond DEA Dude standing there in surfing shorts and a t-shirt, holding a six-pack.

"Don't you have a woman warming your bed right now, Paulson? Why the fuck are you bothering me?"

"Carrie's fine. Great, in fact. But she's having some girl's weekend with her best friend."

"How's Amy doing?"

"Fine. Rehab's helping her with the new arm. But I don't want to talk about the past. Let's talk about today."

"No."

"Try a different answer."

"Fuck, no."

"You were a suckass foot soldier."

"I was never a foot soldier."

"You take orders for shit."

"I give orders, Paulson."

"So now it's Paulson? We're off duty."

"I'm never off duty."

"And that's why I'm here." He plunks the six-pack down, takes one of mine, and opens it with his teeth. "Talk. You rolled a state representative today. I should be bailing you out of jail."

"I know."

"Dead zone in the video surveillance, huh?"

"Lindsay came up with the assailant story on her own. Even set it up by opening the loading dock door and making it look like the guy got away."

"Jesus. She want a job at the CIA?"

"She could run the fucking agency."

I laugh as he hands me another beer. Six is my limit.

Maybe seven tonight.

"I'm not even going to ask why you snapped. That's obvious. But damn, Drew. That was one calculated snap."

"Yep."

"And you jeopardized your entire business for it."

I say nothing.

"I understand the vendetta."

"I don't think you do."

"Then help me understand."

"Why?"

He gives me a look made of granite.

"You really have to ask that? I'm not answering with a list, Drew. I'm asking because watching you throw away everything you've built because you can't keep your fists by your side in the face of an enemy isn't you."

Huh. Word got around fast. "Maybe you don't know me as well as you think."

"Now you sound like some eighteen-year-old recruit who doesn't know the difference between his ass and a hole in the ground."

Because sometimes it feels like I don't.

"Blaine was one of the three attackers."

"I got that loud and clear. Knew that already." He takes a swig of beer and peers at me. "But you're a better strategist."

"I got him in a dead zone."

"That's still sloppy. You know better."

"My temper got the best of me."

"Not good enough, Drew. Still doesn't explain it. I've watched you over the years. You came to Afghanistan like a hollowed-out robot, with a cold, calculating intelligence that masked a rage I've never seen in anyone other than shell-shocked guys with months of IED evasion under their belts. You were fucking scary when we met. *Eager* scary. And with some taming, that mind of yours became our best weapon. You're smarter than this."

I chug the rest of my beer, toss the empty in my recycling container, and reach into the cabinet for reinforcements, finding a bottle of Scotch from my parent's house. I don't drink hard liquor.

I do now.

"It's personal."

"More than personal."

We bathe in the silence between us. The only sound is the trickle of amber fluid from the bottle into a shot glass. I pour two and shove one at him. He holds up a palm.

"No way. I need to get back to Carrie tonight in one piece. Beer's good for me."

I slam back one shot. "Liquid courage."

"You need courage to talk?" Mark's eyebrows shoot up. "This must be bad." He pulls his phone out of his back pocket and starts tapping on the screen.

"Who you texting?" The room is a warm cocoon suddenly, and Mark is my best friend.

"Carrie. Looks like I need to stay here after all."

"No. Go back to your woman. She's waiting in your bed. Go make love and have fun. Smell her neck. Run your hands up her thighs and open them like she's a honeycomb and -- "

Mark grabs my arm with more force than he has any right to use. "Don't talk about Carrie that way."

"Wasn't talking about Carrie."

His grip softens.

"This is about Lindsay," he says under his breath.

"It's always about Lindsay," I say, like someone's ripped my vocal cords in two. "*Always.* But what I did to Blaine today was as much about me as it was about her."

"What's that supposed to mean?"

The words are on the tip of my increasingly numb tongue. I want to say them. *Need* to say them. I've only ever spilled my guts to one person, and she has a Ph.D. and an M.D. after her name and can write a prescription to help me with the obliteration.

My hands shake as I pour a second shot.

"It means I'm a fucking fool."

He puts his hand on mine and carefully removes the shot glass from me with a look that says *enough*. "That was established long ago."

"Then my foolishness expands." The word *foolishness* sounds slurred.

"Man, I've watched you get shitfaced before. After we found that bombed-out village with the kids in the school building..." His voice trails off and he gets the thousand-mile stare I know all too well, except right now, I don't give a fuck about anything.

I tear off onto my deck, where a giggle greets me.

"Drew!" It's Tiffany, my fifty-something cougar neighbor who is wearing a gold bikini at midnight, with a bucket of makeup on her face and a huge pitcher of margaritas on her table. She's smoking a clove cigarette. A gust of wind blows hard just as Mark stomps after me, coming up short when he realizes she's here.

"Oh!" she purrs. "Who's your friend?" Tiffany stands.

She's wearing high heels. Gold ones. They match the string bikini. For a woman my mother's age, she's in great shape.

But definitely not my type.

Mark does that thing with his voice that guys do when they're surprised, but are trying to hide it.

"I'm Tiffany!" she chirps, shuffling over on stilettos and holding out her perfectly manicured hand.

"Mark. Hi."

"Hi there," she says back, giving me a wide-eyed glance. "Drew! You look like a bear ate you and spat you back out."

Mark's lip twitches as he tries not to laugh.

I have to say, normally Tiffany is a fun neighbor to kick back with and have a few drinks, but she's a stereotype of a stereotype.

Tonight, though, the edges of the world are fuzzy and my body's full of adrenaline.

She's still not my type, but that pitcher of margaritas is looking damn fine.

"Been a long day," I say, rubbing my stubbled chin with my hand, then wincing. The knuckles ache from connecting with Blaine's facial bones.

I grin at the memory.

"That's better!" Tiffany giggles. "You look so fierce when you frown!"

"So fierce," Mark mutters.

I glare at him.

"Like that!" Tiffany gushes.

"Smile, Drew," Mark says with a laugh. His eyes dart from me to Tiffany, asking a pretty big question without saying a word. I shake my head *no* imperceptibly, except he catches it.

She doesn't.

"Drew and I hang out all the time. You might call us pitcher buddies!" She shuffles into her apartment suddenly.

"You're nailing her?" Mark asks under his breath as I grab his beer and finish it off. Suddenly, our serious conversation from before is so boring.

A door slams shut inside me.

Good. Let the demons pound on it from the inside. I'm done.

"No. She wishes."

"She's, um..."

"Well preserved."

"You always were the one with tact."

"If I'm tactful, you're Miss Manners."

He guffaws, the sound carrying on the blast of wind that pushes against my t-shirt, making me realize I'm sweating. One more shot and I'm close to snoozing out. I need to hold off.

I shouldn't care.

An image of Lindsay in bed flashes through my blood, hot and coursing through me at a million miles an hour. Naked, wrapped in my arms, her sweet skin against me.

Hard. I'm hard in seconds. This day feels like emotional ping pong.

At the Olympics.

Tiffany re-appears, carrying a third glass, and she pours enormous drinks for the three of us, waving Mark and me over. "Come on! No one wants to drink alone. Especially with such intriguing men just a few feet away. Indulge me?" She gives us a duck face pout.

Mark shrugs and says, "Why not?"

I join them. As I sip my drink, I know I'll regret it in the morning, but I don't care.

I stopped caring the minute Lindsay disappeared with Gentian, who was following my orders, and didn't say another word to me.

"Tiffany is one of my good friends," I say, my body warm and the ocean night air some of the sweetest smelling breezes on the planet. Life is good. I have a place on the ocean, more money than I need, and I run a tight ship. A night here and there of relaxing and having fun should be a part of my life, right?

So why can't I stop thinking about how Lindsay's bare thighs felt in my lap earlier today?

"I am?" Tiffany says, leaning forward. Her top is basically two gold Band-Aids connected by gold string. "I didn't know you felt that way, Drew."

"Sure do, Lindsay," I reply.

Her face freezes into a mask.

"Tiffany," Mark says softly.

"Right. That's what I said." Didn't I?

Mark raises one eyebrow. Tiffany smiles, but it's a cold look.

"What do you do for a living, Mark?" she asks, her hand on his forearm, deciding to make him her target.

"Oh, you know. A little bit of everything."

"Are you a personal trainer like Drew?"

Mark's drink sprays everywhere. "Like Drew?" he chokes, avoiding my eyes, thumping his chest as he clears his airway.

I flex my arm and let my biceps bulge. Why not? I may not want to sleep with Tiffany, but at least she has a healthy appreciation for my presence.

Unlike some other women I know.

Tiffany squeezes my arm and sighs with delight. "Oooo. So strong."

Mark starts gagging.

"Wow! You really swallowed wrong."

He just laugh-chokes.

"I *never* swallow wrong," she says to him with a wink.

I start laughing so hard *I* choke.

We're a pair.

"You two are out of control!" she declares with a laugh, reaching up for the fakest stretch I've ever seen, showing off the fakest pair of breasts I've ever had in my face. They look like two cantaloupes stretched under a skin tarp. "I'm getting so tired," she says as she pretends to yawn along with the stretch.

"Me, too," Mark whispers. "Tired of Drew the personal trainer."

"You guys could easily lift me, huh? Being men who work with their bodies for a living."

I'm thinking Tiffany works with her body for a living, but in a very different way.

My blood pounds like an electromagnetic pulse pointed straight up the coast to Lindsay's father's compound. The same wind that brushes my hair forward is the wind that blows on her face right now. Is she outside, staring at the stars? Looking at the ocean? Sleeping? Thinking of me and touching herself?

I'm already throbbing and have a piece of granite in my pants. Letting my mind wander doesn't take any effort and it feels loose and fine. All the tightness left me long ago, the world swimming before my eyes. I could stare at the moon forever.

I could stare at Lindsay for even longer.

Why'd she lie for me? Creating that fake intruder story was pure genius. No one suspected she was making it up. Plausible deniability was built in. She was quick on her feet and convincing. Blaine could barely argue. In private, I'll be crucified, but in public, he had to play the part of the poor politician attacked by some stranger.

By now, some PR person is giving this a positive spin. Hell, by morning Blaine will be hailed as a hero who took a punch or two to save baby kittens from being killed by Godzilla.

Still does nothing to explain *why*.

Why Lindsay covered for me.

Sure, the satisfaction of watching Blaine bleed was part of it, but not all of it. Lindsay's acting in erratic ways, though she pulled it together for that stage performance next to the senator and Monica. How can she be that composed, and then fall apart in my lap, followed by such strategic thinking in the moment to cover for my lack of impulse control?

She's a paradox.

She's *my* paradox.

"Hey, you two. I don't know about you, but I think this could turn out to be the night of my life," Tiffany says, coming in with a sultry voice and a hand on my ass. I move out of reach. I assume she puts her other one on Mark's butt, because he jumps and moves away from her.

"Sorry. My fiancée would kill me."

"She doesn't have to know."

Mark cuts me a look that could shatter diamonds.

"I have a girlfriend too, Tiffany," I lie.

She frowns. "You never mentioned her before." She's caressing my ass again and moving close, pressing against me as I twist away. She smells so good, and her skin is soft and hairless. I *could* sleep with her. Just once. It would feel nice to disappear into someone else for a few minutes.

But I don't want that.

The only person I want to do that with is Lindsay.

"I don't share much about my personal life," I grind out. Mark's face is so serious. He looks like he'd rather shave his own balls with a rusty razor than stand here with Tiffany and me, talking about threesomes.

Frankly, so would I.

Tiffany sighs, a long, slow sound designed to give Mark and me a chance to change our minds. Her eyes jump between us, and then she drops her head slightly in defeat.

"The good ones are always taken. I hope your women appreciate you."

I cringe inside, but keep my face neutral.

"Right."

Mark gives me a neutral look and starts to walk back inside my apartment. "Carrie's waiting for me." He gives Tiffany a polite smile. "Nice to meet you, Tiffany."

"You got a brother, Mark? Maybe he and I..."

Mark laughs. "My brother's engaged."

"Oh." Tiffany bats her eyelashes at me. "Drew?"

"Only have a sister. And she's married," I add pointedly.

Tiffany giggles. "I don't swing that way."

She clearly swings every way else, though.

"Well," Tiffany says, looking away from us, staring out at the ocean. "My life could be worse than talking to a couple of hot guys and getting rejected. I could have saggy boobs, you know?" She sticks her chest out. "They're good, right? The surgeon says I'm all healed from my lift surgery six weeks ago."

Mark coughs and tries not to look. "They're fine."

Bzzzz.

My back pocket vibrates and I pull out the phone.

Gentian. A routine paperwork question.

I take the opportunity and look at Mark. "Work. We need to go." I nudge my head toward my place. "Bye, Tiffany."

"Bye, Drew. And nice to meet you --"

I close the door and run my hands through my hair while Mark tries to laugh silently.

"Girlfriend? Now you're calling Lindsay your girlfriend? If she's your girlfriend, I'd hate to see what a woman who really hates you looks like, Foster."

I glare. "Fuck off, Paulson."

"Threesome," he gasps. "That's a first."

"Really? Even in the DEA, undercover...?" Mark's worked deep undercover for years.

"Been hit on by guys. Loads of women. Never been offered a threesome, though." He frowns. "Carrie's going to hate hearing this."

I don't even ask why he's telling her. I know his philosophy of relationships. You keep a secret when you need to, or when work requires it. Otherwise, you tell everything, because we already have to keep so many secrets.

Relationships are built on sharing and trust.

Trust.

Right.

Lindsay can't trust me, and I don't blame her.

And I can't share everything with her because I don't have a choice.

"Thanks for the very interesting evening, Foster. I came here to make sure you're okay, and instead I got to be a judge on Best Plastic Surgery in Malibu."

"Don't ever say my jobs aren't intellectually stimulating."

"I think Tiffany's over there intellectually stimulating herself right now," he adds dryly.

"Gross."

But we laugh.

"Tiffany's a nice person. She just has boundary issues."

"Don't fuck her for the wrong reasons, Drew."

I jolt. "Is there a *right* reason? I have zero interest in fucking her."

"Good."

"Why do you care?"

"I don't. But you're so in love with Lindsay, and she's so angry with you, that I can see how crazy it's making you. And when we get crazy, we make bad choices." He grimaces. "I know I have."

"Right." I'm still buzzing, and shutting down. My body twitches, calves spasming. I need to make love with Lindsay, beat off, or go for a ten-mile run.

Preferably all three.

"Look. I came over here to make sure you're okay."

"I'm fine."

"Fine." He lets out a bark of laughter and shakes his head. "Right. Just like we were all *fine* in Afghanistan. *Fine* is the stupidest word when it comes to describing emotional states."

"You sound like my psychologist."

"How *is* Dr. Diamante?" The question isn't casual. I know what he's telling me. Not asking.

Telling.

"Wouldn't know. Haven't had to see her in a while."

"Might want to give her a call."

"Might not."

His nostrils flare. It's posturing. He's not my commanding officer any longer. In fact, I'm his boss. And my personal life and emotional state are none of Mark's business. Nice of him to care, but he needs to butt the fuck out.

He sighs and reaches into his pocket, jangling his car keys. "Do what you want."

"I always do."

"But -- "

I groan.

"But you almost got yourself fired today. Expect a text from the senator."

"Already got one."

"He's pissed. Rightly so. Everyone's pretending to accept Lindsay's fake story about an 'attacker,' but that's her one shot. Another mess like this and you're toast."

"You mean *she* is."

"Yeah." His voice turns sad. "Yeah. She's in an impossible bind."

I flinch. He frowns, puzzled, then pulls back, blinking hard.

"Sorry. Poor choice of words."

A vision of Lindsay bound and tied by those animals makes my blood race. The twitchiness overcomes all the alcohol in my system and I start to breathe hard. Grabbing a glass, I pour myself water from the pitcher in my fridge and guzzle it down.

Mark just watches me.

"You really love her."

"Of course." My voice comes out like ice chips, one piece per syllable. "You knew that."

"It's one thing to be told something. It's very different to watch it."

"That obvious?"

"You might as well wear her panties on your head."

I'm in the middle of a swallow and come out choking, hard. That image is way better than my previous one, so I'll go with that.

"Doubt the senator would appreciate it," I cough out.

"You'd get fired. Surprised you're not. And if you keep it up, Drew, you'll be arrested for assault."

"You're playing the puritan with me? The guy who broke into his own father's motorcycle club compound so he could rescue his brother's girlfriend from a drug dealer who planned to take her virginity to cure his HIV/AIDS?"

He nods slowly. "When you put it that way, I'm a hypocrite."

"When I put it ANY way, you're fucking crazy."

He claps me on the shoulder. "We both are. We know that. Always have been, especially since Afghanistan."

"And since both of us had parents who died in mysterious car crashes."

Mark's eyes go dark. "And that," he spits out. The coincidence was too pat to be anything but a careful targeting. Mark was already my commanding officer and delivered the news, followed by his own hollow story that mimicked what happened to my mom and dad, only it was his mother and stepfather.

Grief has a funny way of going underground when you're in battle. They sent me home for the funeral. I grieved with my sister in private, handled a few legalities, and requested to be sent back to the front lines.

Lindsay was still on the Island.

I had no one to talk to back home.

Combat was a better place to express my emotions. Sniper training proved cathartic.

"Between my parents, your parents, and Lindsay's brake line failure, looks like we've got someone in high places targeting all of us."

"Us?" Mark grabs a glass and fills it with water, our conversation obviously not over. "You think I'm still some kind of target?" His eyes flicker with worry, then settle back into a blank stare.

"Not sure."

"You think Carrie -- "

"You live next door to your brother now, right?"

"Right."

"He's good?" Mark knows what I am really asking.

"He'd shred anyone who tried to touch Carrie or Allie. No training, but solid instincts."

"He looking for a job?"

Mark laughs, tipping his head back, setting the glass down. "No. Chase has his life planned. No need to draw him into this."

"And your dad?" Mark's biological father was one of the deepest undercover CIA agents in agency history. He'd become a motorcycle club president in Southern California and had been instrumental in the assassination of the biggest international drug lord in U.S. history.

El Brujo.

Chase's girlfriend had actually killed El Brujo, but credit went to Galt, to protect her.

"Galt's gone. Well hidden, far from here."

"Good. That's where he should be."

"Don't want to talk about Galt."

"Don't want to talk about Lindsay," I say, mimicking him.

He shrugs. "We need to figure out who's behind all this, and if that means getting close to her to get info, you might have to do it."

"Like you did with Carrie when you were trying to get her father convicted?"

He winces.

"I take that back."

"You damn well better. I'm not jeopardizing my relationship with her for the sake of a mission."

Cold eyes meet mine.

"Then you're not the soldier I once knew."

"Maybe that soldier wasn't as good as you thought."

I grunt.

"Drew." He says my name like it's a threat.

I turn away, going into my bedroom, ignoring him. He doesn't follow, and by the time I'm in running shorts, a t-shirt, and have my hydropack water system on, Mark's gone. I look out my front window just in time to see him climb into a giant black SUV, one I recognize from Harry's security detail.

A vague sense of unease fills my pores.

Time to run it off.

CHAPTER EIGHT

I live six miles from The Grove, but it's like living in another world. The apartments on the beach up the coast are nice and way above my old pay grade in the military, but as I pound out the miles on dirt paths and paved roads, dipping into the beach sand here and there, I feel the money *change*.

You can smell money in California. It smells like a freshly-watered green lawn.

Having studied topography and boundary maps of the three square miles around The Grove, I know exactly how to get on the estate grounds without being noticed.

Which enrages me. My guys should be better.

I trained them to do better.

"Gentian!" I bark into my ear piece. "Jesus Fucking Christ, I just snuck onto the grounds. What the hell are the -- "

A red laser from a rifle sight bounces right between my eyes.

"Not good enough," I grunt. "Twenty seconds is all they need. Do better."

"We just turned the sight on to make a point, sir. Had you the entire time."

Good man.

"Fair enough."

"There a problem, sir?"

"No. Just coming in to check out the terrain and reinforce security."

"They're safe, sir. We've got it covered."

Apparently, they do.

He comes out of the bushes to my right, wearing dark, casual clothes, gun belt loose around his waist, no attempt made to hide it.

"Lindsay's here," he informs me.

"Where else would she be?" I bark.

"There was some question about whether she'd accompany her mother to New York for a charity event."

"Oh."

"Her mother declined. Said Lindsay's not ready for it."

I snort. "Monica's PR people probably told her the numbers wouldn't move in the positive direction."

"I gathered as much."

Gentian's looking at Lindsay's window, which is dark.

"No sign of those bastards or their operatives?"

"None."

"You double-checked the backgrounds of all my men?"

"Yes. They're clean."

My bladder has been screaming for attention since mile three. I walk around a bush, void it, and come back to find him gone.

"Sir?" My earpiece crackles. "Change of the team for the new shift. If you need me, we can meet up again inside."

"No. Go do the shift switch." I stare at the pale grey glass, the nighttime sky reflected in her window, the sheer curtains behind it wispy, decorative nothingness. We've added thick curtains designed to help with gunshots. While the glass is bulletproof, it's not perfect. I make a mental note to check on additional infrastructure issues we can upgrade on the house.

And then the curtains part, Lindsay appearing in the moonlight, wearing a gauzy nightgown, her hair down and loose around her shoulders.

My mouth goes dry.

My heart stops.

My body burns.

She's looking out at the ocean, the waves gorgeous under the moonlight, the sound so soothing it's a lullaby. I don't look, instead taking the rare chance to observe her without her knowing. In profile, she's ethereal, the long line of her straight nose leading to a full upper lip I've kissed a thousand times, and want to kiss a million more.

Her flowing blond hair tumbles down around her shoulders like it's eager to caress her, as if it knows how privileged it is to be part of her body. She tucks a loose strand behind her ear and sighs, leaning against the window pane on her hands, blinking as she breathes slowly. Her eyebrows turn down and the worry lines appear on her face.

She's too young to have worry lines like that.

I want to smooth them away.

It's my job to protect her, but it's my life's mission to make her feel like she never needs to be protected. To make her feel so safe she never has to worry again.

As her forehead presses against the glass, she closes her eyes, long lashes resting softly against the fine bones of her cheeks. Lindsay is the only woman I've ever truly wanted. I've been with others, but that wasn't real – it was just the momentary relief of not being alone. Fleeting and simple, it left me unfulfilled. Unsatisfied. Wanting more, but always with someone else.

With the woman I'm staring at right now.

A single tear rolls down her cheek and my throat tightens. I want to wipe it away. I want to bury her cheek in my shoulder and hold her until she doesn't hurt any more.

Her eyes snap open and meet mine.

Drew, she says, her mouth forming my name.

And then she closes her eyes and lifts her hand, pressing her palm against the glass.

That's all the invitation I need.

The sprint around the house and through the kitchen door is greeted by various security team members calling out, "Sir," snapping to attention like the ex-military members they are. Rank doesn't count here.

Being their boss does.

I'm up the stairs two at a time until I stop in front of her door, two guys watching me, turning away when they are certain of my identity. My heart's slamming in my chest like I'm slapping it. I curl my fingers into a fist and knock.

"Come in," she says in a tiny voice that feels like tears.

I open the door without looking at her, pivoting to close it slowly, turning the lock without discussion. I know why she invited me.

So does she.

Four years of wondering are about to end.

Four years of trying to atone are about to be redeemed.

She stands in front of the window, turned toward me, eyes wide and glistening. A small, dim light next to her bed is the only way I can see her, the moonlight behind her crowded out by the curtains, which slowly swish as she steps forward, abruptly cutting off the outdoor light.

Her nightgown is open at the neck, an oddly feminine article that isn't the norm for her. Then again, what's normal for Lindsay?

She moves like sunshine, like stardust, her feet bare and sweet, her arms at her sides.

"Drew," she whispers.

By the time she starts to say another word, she's in my arms and my mouth is on hers, silencing her. I'm brutal, and I don't care. I need to take this kiss. I need to pull it out of her, gasp by gasp, moan by moan. I need to make her give it to me until she begs me to stop.

Until she's ready for more.

Until her pain is gone.

"You taste like sweat and alcohol," she says with a laugh.

"Guilty of both." I roll my lips, biting them. "Alcohol's long out of my system from the run. That okay?" I want her to know I'm clear-headed.

She shrugs and frowns. "I didn't – God, Drew, that was close. Why did you beat him up?"

She wants to talk.

Huh.

Okay...

"How could I not?" The words are wrenched out of me, pulled like a tug-of-war, scraped across my tongue. I cool my jets. That kiss fired them up. "That bastard was right there, Lindsay. He fucking *dared* to talk to you. He doesn't deserve to breathe the same air. Not from a continent away."

Her eyes search my face, asking for something. I don't know what.

"Thank you."

"For hitting him? No need to thank me. I didn't do it for you. I did it for me."

"You did it for both of us. When I saw him talking to you, some part of me died inside."

"You've had more than enough parts beaten and broken. You don't need more."

"But I can't forget."

Her face burns with revenge.

A prickly heat starts at the base of my spine and shoots up. "Lindsay, stay out of this."

"Stay out of what?"

"Whatever you're planning."

She gives me a hard look.

But doesn't deny it.

I try a different tack.

"We can work together."

"What?" She's genuinely surprised.

"Together. This is bigger than both of us. Getting back at them is, too. You stole my gun, Lindsay. You're afraid my guys and I can't protect you. You're trying to be a lone wolf. You don't have to. Don't you see? That's why I'm here. Why my guys are here."

"I thought you were here because my father hired you."

"That's the surface reason."

She narrows her eyes, studying me, all traces of crying gone.

"I still don't know who to trust. Mom and Daddy said I did well today. Mom was horrified by the strange 'accident' you and Blaine had."

I let out a grunt.

"And they don't want me on any more campaign stops for a while."

"How do you feel about that?"

"Relieved."

I would be, too. None of this is what she wants.

"But I have this big feeling of 'now what?' hanging over me."

"So do I," I tell her, voice low, body language clear.

Her face turns, looking out the window, but she steps into my body space again. I wrap my arms around her. She sinks into me. The heat of her skin makes her so soft. So yielding.

"I've missed you," I say.

"I was a complete bitch to you earlier," she says with a cold laugh. But she doesn't move out of my arms.

"That's fine. It turns me on."

She smiles and shakes her head fast, like she can't believe me. "Pervert."

I just shrug.

We go silent. As seconds tick by, the stakes get higher. I did punch Blaine today. That was a tactical move motivated by pure revenge. I need to up my game. Planned attacks are one thing.

Impulse will get me killed.

Or worse.

Acting on impulse could get Lindsay harmed.

That is unacceptable.

I bury my nose in Lindsay's hair and inhale.

The moonlight shimmers as she pulls the curtains closed. Without another word, she turns, reaches up, and presses the full length of her body against mine. Long and languid, like hot caramel being poured up my body, she seals the embrace with a kiss.

Not just any kiss.

Her lips open and her tongue insists on getting my full attention.

Which isn't a problem.

At *all*.

We kiss, a slow, wet connection that makes my sweaty shirt soak into her. Lindsay doesn't seem to care. Her fingers thread through the wet hair at the nape of my neck. Her little sounds of pleasure drive me further. Soon, my hands are on her breasts and she's grabbing my shoulders, one hand riding down to my ass.

This escalated fast.

Thank God.

"What you did was so powerful," she gasps against my mouth. Pulling back, her eyes blaze as we look at each other. "I haven't felt that protected in -- "

"In four years."

"Yes." She doesn't look away. She doesn't get mad. She doesn't look uncertain.

Instead, she kisses me again.

"Plus," she adds as she comes up for air, the electrical charge between us almost visible, "he didn't see it coming.

Those assholes are taunting me. They think they have all the control." A calculating smile turns those red lips into something diabolical. "But they have no idea what's coming."

"If anything's coming, I want it to be you, first. Then us, together," I groan in her ear, blowing lightly until she shivers. I get serious. "If you'll have me."

"I'm ready. That's why I asked you up here. More than ready," she whispers. Shoulders back, body language clear, this is a more confident Lindsay. Punching Blaine turns out to have been a move that puts me at a strategic advantage. Not against the scarves.

But in terms of my heart.

Lindsay trusts me now.

Enough to let me into her body, at least.

"You're in control," I tell her, stripping out of my running shirt. She gasps at my naked chest, flattening her palm against my pecs, sliding down.

"Sorry for the sweat," I apologize.

"Don't. It's hot." She reaches down and bites one of my nipples lightly.

"Hot as in sexy?" I hiss into her ear, picking her up and covering her body with mine. "Or hot as in heat."

"Both."

"I like both." She touches the ear she bit the other day, eyebrows knitting with regret.

"I want everything, Drew. Everything. Make me feel. You already make me want you." A gentle kiss on my ear punctuates her words.

"I do?"

"God, yes, you do."

"Lindsay, I don't want you."

She tenses.

"I crave you. I *need* you. You're like a drug and I'm an addict. You're an obsession that won't stop looping through my mind. I wish all I felt was want. This would be so much easier. Every second I'm not touching you is like being tortured."

"Then stop torturing yourself." She shimmies out of her nightgown.

She is completely naked underneath. Not even panties.

"Oh." I swallow, throat suddenly dry. My running shorts tent. She looks down at my erection.

"Take those off."

"Are you sure?"

"Are you going to ask me that every step of the way?"

"What do you want, Lindsay?" I comply with her request. It's the least I can do.

We're naked before each other. But are we truly stripped bare?

Her shoulders rise and fall faster, breasts pert and perfect, her breath quickening as she takes me in and says, "I want you to shut up and make love to me, Drew. I want to claim what's ours. I want what we lost four years ago."

"I'm not sure I can give all that to you." I step forward and touch her arms, pulling her close, hip to hip.

"Then let's at least try," she rasps in my ear.

"That I can do, with tremendous pleasure."

Or die trying.

CHAPTER NINE

This time, the kiss holds expectation tinged with belief, the very real feeling that this is about to unfold. We're naked, pressed together in a tangle of skin and limbs, hair and fingers, tongues finding secrets between us and making them come alive, exposing them to the air where they evaporate.

She tastes like salty sweet hope, like an unleashed temptress who finally gets to test the world, who can push and see how powerful she really is. I am not about to be an obstacle as Lindsay finally, exquisitely, reaches for what she wants.

Wholeness.

We can find it together, I know, as her hair tickles my jaw, our abs brushing together, her belly going tight as I cup one breast and revel in the fullness. It's light and heavy, a globe of agile heat, and my fingertip skims the nipple, making her moan.

My cock pushes against her thigh, her legs shifting as I cradle her jaw with my other hand and kiss her until I can't tell the difference between her breath and mine.

"You taste perfect. You taste like everything, Lindsay. I've wanted to kiss you a million times a day, every day, for four years. How do you do it?" Before she can answer, I kiss her again, a slow, languid kiss that takes its time, as if it's separate from us, an entity that has its own agenda.

"Do what?" she asks, breathless. I slide my hand down her ribs, the sweet curve of her waist, the swell of her hip, then forward and lower, one finger sliding to a point that makes her gasp and cling to me, shuddering with pleasure.

"Taste so good." I kiss her shoulder, touching her with slow, wet circles. Her knees bend and she gives me more of her weight as her lips part. I kiss my way down, until it's my turn to bend my knees, lowering myself before her.

I worship at the altar of Lindsay.

"Spread your legs," I order.

"What?" Her voice is hazy, a million miles away.

I use my hands to move her. She threads her fingers in my hair as I reach up, my tongue finding what I seek, my hands cupping her ass as she moans and widens her legs, standing before me as I kneel.

This.

Ah, *this*.

She tastes so much better right here. Her mouth is an appetizer, her nipples a garnish.

This is a main course.

"Drew, I -- " Lindsay sucks in a huge breath and tightens as I seek warmth, one of my fingers inside her, the sound of appreciation that she makes all I need. I want to make her feel good. I want to make her let go. I want to be the one person in the entire world who gives her what she deserves.

Permission to be herself.

Every breath I take as she falls deeper and deeper into a place no one – not even I – can touch, makes me love her more. My hands and mouth can perform magic on her skin, but can they work to mend the years of hurt?

All I can do is try.

And try.

And never, *ever* stop trying.

She pulls away, but I tighten my hold, determined to make her lose herself so she can find herself again, bigger and better than before. There is nothing in the world more honorable than having someone choose to be raw and vulnerable with you. Nothing. Having Lindsay trust me enough to shatter and buck, to writhe and groan, is a gift.

"I want you, Drew. Deep inside me -- " She gasps, her throat closed by the spasm that wraps my fingers in a tight clench, her sweet flesh swelling under my lips and tongue, her body swaying above me.

She folds. I follow. I chase her down, down, down to the ground where she quietly burns as climax after climax bring her to ecstasy, my singular goal to keep her in that place where all she knows is sensation and goodness, where her fine bones and supple flesh are the entire world, and where she can only say my name as if it were the singular lifeline she has to keep her tied to reality.

I'm doing this for her.

Me.

But she lets me.

Emotion pours through me, combined with arousal, catching my throat off-guard, making my eyes pinprick, my heart slamming in my chest like nothing I've ever felt before. I spiral inward as Lindsay's hands cover mine, her thigh against my mouth as she twists, her voice a pale hush that says, "Oh, God, I need you."

She sits up and pulls me to her, the taste of her willing surrender now on her lips, too, as we say so much with anything *but* words. Soon, I'm over her, the bed next to us, looming like a sentry, the floor more than enough for our connection, our linking, our reunion.

I've never been inside her before.

She has to ask. I won't come uninvited.

"Please," she whispers, the vibration low and soft. I feel it against my abs, her request diffusing out from her skin as well as in words. "Please, Drew. Make love to me. I want you in me. I want you everywhere."

Stage fright isn't my thing. Unlike other guys in my unit, I never froze when the pressure was on. And that's not happening right now. It's not.

Really.

But I lean down on one elbow and take my other hand, cupping her jaw. We look at each other without walls. Without pretense. But the past is there, hovering, watching.

It needs to see us together.

The past cannot be put to rest, put in its place, until it knows we've healed.

Our kiss lingers, the seconds chasing away all the fears, the worries, the condemnation and the insecurities. As we kiss, she moves under me, widening her legs.

"I'm on the pill," she whispers, removing that concern. The comment brings me back to reality, and I suddenly am hyperaware of every aspect of my body. The cold push of air as she breathes against my sweat-soaked skin. How the moonlight curls into the grooves of muscle in my forearm. The way the curtains billow and make Lindsay's eyes look like wet lace. The view of my hip against her ass cheek, resting together like two old friends.

How her perfect breasts settle against her chest when she's flat on her back, her nipples tight like little crowns.

"You're my queen," I blurt out. Her eyes dance with amusement, the arousal still there.

"That's one of the weirdest things I've ever heard you say," she replies, her fingertips giving me butterfly strokes up and down my side, halting at my hip, then moving with a bold perfection until she has me wrapped in her palm, all fire and rigid need.

"But you are," I groan as she strokes me.

"Make love to me, Drew," she says, taking me in. The tip is at her entrance, waiting, holding back as I move over her, knees on either side of her nude body, our fervent eagerness making us both shake. She is ready.

I've been ready forever.

And now it's time.

Second by second, with aching slowness, I enter her. Lindsay looks at me the entire time, our eyes locked, and as I move into her, it is like finding holy ground without knowing it. I've stumbled across a portal into a place where nothing else matters. Just her. Just me.

Just us.

Just *this*.

"Oh," she moans, the tiny hairs on her legs going to gooseflesh, the bumps shimmying up her leg from shin to hip, rippling. I feel it against my own hair-covered legs and I cannot describe it. The sensation is excruciatingly unique. It's chilly and exciting, in contrast to the warm, wet glory of being inside her. I sink down, deep, and she widens for me.

"Come into me, Drew," she says in my ear, licking my neck. "Come as deep as you can, until you touch the part of me I've kept from everyone else."

For a split second, I freeze, a single image from that night hitting me full force. No. No. I am not going to let it contaminate this homecoming.

Fuck, no.

They do not get to destroy this. I can't change the past, but letting thoughts of that hideous night touch one single second of making love with Lindsay isn't happening.

It takes everything I have not to whisper the word *no*.

And that *no* isn't for Lindsay.

"Drew?" She touches my cheek with one manicured finger and I twitch, jumping out of my own thoughts. "Are you okay?"

"I'm better than okay, baby." I lose myself in the kiss, her warmth infusing me, coming back into the amazing moment. "You make me better." I slowly pull back, then move in her, the feeling superb.

She makes a breathy sound of pleasure. "I love you," she says, eyes closed, a smile on her lips.

Fierce, pure love shoots through me like someone blasted a cannon filled with blood in my veins. "I love you too, Lindsay. God, I truly do. Let me show you."

"You are showing me, Drew. Let's show each other."

And we do.

The build-up comes fast, with lightning speed, until we're all moans and sighs, our names cried out and she's so slippery, so wet for me, until all I am is her. We come together, Lindsay clinging to me with a shuddering finality that makes me explode, carried off by waves, the privilege of letting go with her a kind of love I didn't know we could share.

Sweaty, sated, and breathing hard, I collapse onto her, still in her. She jolts and I move, just enough, face buried in the hot mess of her tangled hair. A sense of accomplishment, of pride, radiates out from my core to my hipbones, my quads, my glutes, up my spine, making me heady and dizzy.

I did it.

We did it.

Four years of pain and heartbreak, of recovery and hiding – gone.

Four years of the unknown, of mourning what we lost, of strategy and hope, of bitterness and regret – gone.

Her breath goes slow, my own steadying as the hot rasp of everything we just shared cycles back against my skin, feeding

Λ Harmless Little Ruse

me, nourishing us. I pull up to say how full my heart is, how much she means to me, and how I will never, ever let her go.

Our eyes meet.

And she bursts into tears.

CHAPTER TEN

A larm replaces the sense of completion, my gut tearing to shreds as I feel wetness from her tears against my shoulder.

"Oh, my God, Lindsay," I say gruffly, sitting up, getting off her. "Did I hurt you? What's wrong? I didn't mean to -- "

She grabs me and sits up, burying her face in my chest, her arms wrapping around me. My heart beats so hard it's like I'm punching her in the face.

"No, no," she says, muffled. "I'm not crying because of pain."

"Well...I..." Shit. I can barely say the next few words, but I have to. "Was the sex that bad?"

She half-coughs, half-laughs, half-sobs. "No! No! It was amazing. You're amazing. We're amazing together."

I let out my breath. Didn't realize I was holding it.

"I don't know why I'm crying!" she confesses, her mouth against my nipple. The vibration feels weird, chaotic and out of order. I swear it makes my heart skip a beat.

I cough. It's instinctive, but my rhythm resumes.

"It's okay. Shhhhh," I say, soothing her, brushing her wet hair off her face, kissing the salty tears.

"It's not okay. I've been such a bitch to you. I couldn't trust you."

I choke, the air shooting out of me, surprised by her words. "What? That's why you're crying?" We're naked and sweaty, covered in each other's slick, and she's crying after the most phenomenal emotional moment of my life because she's been mean to me?

This can't be real.

"Y-y-yes," she whimpers. "I didn't know I could love someone this much. I knew I loved you, Drew, but not like this!" Her little fists rub her tears away. She sniffles. "And you're the first person I've ever asked to do that. To be inside me. I didn't know it would feel like this."

"Like what?" I prod gently, trying to understand. I run the tip of my nose across the crown of her head, breathing in the tropical scent of her shampoo, her hair impossibly soft.

"Like I've been living in half the world, not knowing the rest existed."

I'm dumbfounded.

What the hell do you say in response to *that*?

"That's exactly how I feel," I confess, tightening my hold on her. She wiggles closer, into my lap. We link ourselves, breathing as one, until I untangle our bodies and bring her to the bed. An afterthought, for sure, but she relaxes in my arms when we're under the covers, as if she feels safer.

Covered.

Not quite so exposed.

Only our naked bodies underneath the surface know the truth.

Her tears subside. I understand them now.

"I never told anyone who the fourth man was in that video."

"You didn't? Not a single person? Not even your dad?"

She shakes her head. The admission makes me feel good for some reason.

"Why not?" I gently ask. Prodding this truth out of her feels like it's a fulcrum that allows me to crack open the future.

"Because I couldn't believe it. Couldn't believe you'd do that to me. Just...let them."

"I didn't."

"I know. Even in the face of what looked so obvious, I just...knew. I knew you wouldn't do that to me, but God, Drew, it hurt so much." She tightens her hold on me, her body starting to tremble. When you're pressed naked, toe to shoulder, against someone, you feel everything.

"So you had to hold two truths inside you at the same time. Two truths that couldn't co-exist.'

She jolts, her head popping up, eyes beseeching. "Yes. Exactly. How did you know?"

"Because that's what I hoped for four years. That some part of you trusted me enough to know that the obvious couldn't be true."

"It's the same with that picture they texted me. The one with you and part of my red scarf."

Breathe, Foster. *Breathe.*

Bzzz.

"Reality," I sigh, letting out a sound of relief that I pretend is frustration as I search for my phone. Lindsay ends the sound by kissing me. The sound turns, twisting into a decidedly different groan.

"Thank you," she says.

"No need." I kiss her forehead. We just breathe together, so much unsaid.

We have time.

Bzzz.

Or not.

"Besides," I add, standing grudgingly, searching for my clothes, knowing the phone's in there somewhere. "This time, you're not stealing my weapon."

The laughter pours out of her like a contagion and she sits up, pulling me back to the bed. It's hopeless. I can't not laugh. I curl up around her, cocooning her, arms and legs tucked in.

She's shaking in my arms, the vibration making my skin tingle.

It's good to hear her laugh.

It's even better to laugh together.

"I'm sorry," she finally gasps. "I couldn't trust you."

I stop laughing.

Her skin is dewy and warm, a light trace of heat along the pores making her flush.

"Talk to me," I say. "Tell me more."

She sighs, a little sound of vulnerability. It makes my throat tighten. That's the sound someone makes when they are about to be real.

I've wanted nothing more than the real Lindsay this whole time.

Thank God she's finally here.

"Drew," she says, her hand snuggling on my bare chest, the lines of her tendons standing out as she moves. "They broke me. Ripped me apart – literally." Her thighs shift and my shoulders tighten.

"I know."

"When I woke up, it was like I'd been turned inside out. I was nothing but pain. The physical pain subsided, eventually. But in some ways that was worse. *Not* having my body hurt."

Oh, man. I know where she's going with this.

Because I've been there.

Only she doesn't know that.

"Because then all that was left was the pain in my mind. And that was a different kind of agony. Worse."

I squeeze her gently. I have to. If I don't hold on, I'll fall off the edge of the world.

She's giving words to *my* pain. *My* madness. Four years ago, she wasn't the only one those assholes destroyed, but she doesn't know that.

And I can't tell her.

My skin erupts into a furious tingle, as if my blood's trying to escape but hits the wall of skin and can't. That same mind that contains all the insanity of being brutalized is the one that manages to love her, too. I'm ten thousand Drews inside a single body right now.

And only one of me can listen to her.

"Nothing I thought about stopped the intrusions," she whispers. Her breathing is even, and she's resting against me, skin to skin. *Trust.* She's trusting me. Lindsay is opening herself to me. She just gave me her body. Invited me to share it. Welcomed me into her so we could find pieces of ourselves we lost four years ago.

Now she's inviting me into her heart. Into her mind.

Into that inner space where we protect our core.

I don't take this lightly.

I am honored.

"Nothing."

I make a sound of comfort. I don't know what to say.

"They medicated me into oblivion." She snorts. "I didn't care. It was easier to take the little cup of pills twice a day than to argue. Easier to crawl into bed and sleep. Even though I had bad dreams." She shivers. I absorb all her pain. I take in her memories.

It hurts.

It heals.

I don't have a choice.

"I'm so sorry," I say, rubbing her shoulder, staring at the moon. If I look at her, I might lose the pieces of myself I just found.

"And so," she continues, breathless now. It's as if she's relieved to finally talk. I close my eyes and take in the way air passes through her throat. When she speaks, the vibration of her voice touches every cell in me.

"And so I just lived like I was hollow. Insert medication. Hope it dulled the memories. Wait." She sits up, eyes finding mine. They're impossibly wide, big and pleading, needing more of me. "Do you know what that's like?"

Yes.

"No," I lie. "I can't imagine."

"The hardest part was thinking you had let them hurt me. Or worse – that you were in on it."

That snaps me out of my own reactions. "For the rest of my life, until the day I die, I'll regret that I couldn't stop them. *Couldn't.*"

"I know."

"No, Lindsay, I don't think you do."

Her face morphs. Emotion flickers in ten thousand licks across the fine bones of her face. The moon conspires against me, giving her a grey shadow as clouds cover the light, making her eerie. Dangerous.

My heart seizes.

"You cannot fathom how hard it was to be drugged and -- " Helpless.

I cannot say that fucking word.

" -- and unable to stop them."

"I can now. Now that I know the truth. They hurt you too, Drew."

I jerk. What's she implying? Does she know the full truth?

I stay silent. Don't give away a thing. She'll reveal what she knows, and I can make sure I don't tip my hand.

"They drugged you. Made it so you couldn't stop them. And that blood on you in the picture – they beat you up, didn't they? I know."

93

I hold my breath. What *else* does she know? Because yes, they beat me.

But they did worse, too.

"You told me," she continues. "I believe you. I rewatched the video."

"You what?"

She shrugs, her breast sliding down my rib, nipple peaking. "I had to. After you told me what happened, I went online and watched it."

"You found the video online?"

She makes a huff of laughter, a sad sound. "I have my ways, as you know."

"I thought we'd put a stop to that," I say tightly.

She bats at my chest. "You can't outsmart me."

I snort. Her eyebrows go up. She kisses me.

As her lips brush mine, I find the passion is gone. In its place there is a sense of regret. Of peace. A kind of sad acceptance that the past has damaged us, but somehow we've found our way back to each other. We're scarred and battered, bruised and broken, but we're together again.

That is its own miracle.

Bzzzz.

I groan. "My phone." I stand, searching again for my clothes, finding the damn device and checking.

Seven a.m. staff meeting in two hours. You want me to get a suit for you? Senator Bosworth plans to be there, Gentian texts me.

I should be worried.

I'm not.

Worst case, he fires my company from covering Lindsay.

Best case, he yells at me for punching Blaine.

There is no option for being praised.

"Who's the text from?"

"Gentian." I walk closer to the window, careful not to make my body viewable from outside. The pre-dawn light makes the sky a strange color. I'm wiped and wired at the same time. A long, hard day followed by too many beers, a six-mile run, and a lovemaking session that qualifies as the best of my entire life.

All the good and bad in the world crammed into the same single day.

"Hey," Lindsay whispers, coming up from behind me and wrapping her arms around my waist. "Everything okay? Is Silas texting because there's a problem?"

Understatement of the year.

"Your dad plans to attend our seven a.m. staff meeting."

"But he's in D.C."

I shrug. "Maybe he's on video feed. Or maybe his schedule changed. My little stunt with Blaine might have worse consequences than I anticipated."

She sighs, hot breath tickling my shoulder blade. Pressing her cheek against my back, she melts into me. "They don't tell me anything. I'm relieved now, though."

"Relieved?" I text back a quick *yes* to Gentian, then put the phone down and press my palms against her hands. Having her touch me is an anchor.

"I think they're happy I performed the part. They're done with me, for a week or two at least. I smiled, I was vibrant, I played the good daughter in a highly public role. I'm not some sex-crazed kinky deviant who is an embarrassment to the good senator."

"Lindsay," I protest, my voice low with anger. "No one thinks that."

A bitter laugh vibrates against my back. "Everyone thinks that, Drew. Daddy said he couldn't believe I let it happen." I rotate her around so she faces me.

"He said that to you? I remember Harry saying it to *me*." Fury turns the room a dark shade of red, her sadness making me protective..

She blinks rapidly as she struggles to remember. "Oh. Maybe that's when I was eavesdropping on you two."

"When you were what? Excuse me?"

An impish smile stretches her lips and she shrugs. "It was my first day back. I was desperate."

All I can do is sigh.

"At least I didn't punch a California state representative," she needles. "My only saving grace is that the news media cycle is so fast. Everyone cares more about a boy in a tiger display at a zoo than they do about me now. The media is fickle. The more boring I am, the better for Daddy."

"You're anything but boring."

"You know what I mean."

My temper flares up. "Yeah. I do. And I hate it. You're so much more than a pretty face on a stage, filling a spot on a politician's checkbox."

"Am I? Are you sure?"

I tighten my hold, my thighs pressing into her hips, my cock dragging across that soft skin right above her mons. As much skin as possible needs to connect between us. If I touch her enough, I can erase time, right?

I know I can't.

But I'll give it my best shot.

"I'm sure." I kiss her forehead, then both cheeks, finally settling a sweet kiss on her lips. "More than sure. You deserve your own life, Lindsay."

"I don't know what that even means."

"You've been home barely a week. Give it time. Settle in and give yourself space."

She grabs me, hard. "I don't want space. Not from you."

"Present company excepted."

She laughs, her eyes flicking up to catch mine. "I've missed you. Not just you. Not just your presence. I've missed this." Her palm flattens against my back, sliding up my spine as if counting the bones. "The easy way we have with each other."

"Me, too." Emotion overwhelms me. She cannot possibly know how deeply I've ached for her. Four years.

Four fucking years.

"All that anger, Drew. I was so hurt, and I hated you so much for betraying me. Knowing now that I was wrong makes me feel so ashamed. I'm sorry."

I pull her back from me by the shoulders, my fingers gripping her hard enough to make her yelp. "Don't you ever say that!" I hiss, the explosive emotion in me set off like an IED. "Never. I never, ever want you to feel shame for anything those bastards did to you. How you felt about me is understandable. They planted that feeling in you. They orchestrated the betrayal by your friends. They set us *both* up. You have nothing to be ashamed of."

I'm shaking her. I can't stop. Some deep part of me thinks I can shake the shame out of her.

She rips herself away from me and stands a yard away, mouth twisted in fury. "I know that! I know it up here!" She taps her temple. Then her hand moves over her deliciously creamy skin, settling just above a naked breast, right over her heart. "But I don't know it *here*."

I cross the space and press my palm flat over hers.

"I do," I whisper. "I know."

Her eyes fill with tears.

And I almost tell her.

In Afghanistan, there was an incident. IED, ambush on a high mountain road, and in the middle of the attack one of our jeeps went down a three-hundred-foot cliff. The driver managed to jump out, but the guys in back were lost. As it tipped before my eyes, the passenger door had a hand.

Yeah, a hand. The hand shot out through the open window and I grabbed it as the soldier jumped out, bracing his legs on something inside to get some force. Our eyes met.

It could have gone either way. Life or death. Success or failure.

His body smashed against the edge of the window, ribs squished like thick toothpaste being squeezed out of a tube. He later had massive internal bleeding but my grip on his forearm – hard enough to dislocate his shoulder – kept him from tipping over that edge.

The jeep nearly dragged him down.

Impulse and training and sheer will kept him alive. The jeep almost took me down, too.

And right now, Lindsay looks an awful lot like a random hand poking out of an open window on a bombed jeep that is about to go over a cliff.

We are naked, standing before each other, hands on her heart. The look on her face says so much.

Rescue me.

Love me.

Don't leave.

I'm damaged.

Don't shame me.

I'm sorry.

"How do you know?" she asks. "How do you know what I should or shouldn't feel?" Her voice is so soft. There's no challenge. No anger. Just a gentle request that I answer the mystery of the universe.

No pressure, right?

"I don't claim to know you better than you know yourself, Lindsay." I look down at our hands, together against her fine skin. "But I know that if you harbor shame inside you for how you've treated me, let it go. Let every fucking drop of it go. That's not a burden you need to carry. All the shame is on John, Stellan and Blaine."

She flinches at their names.

I reach to her chin and tip it up, so her eyes meet mine. "You are my world. My soul can release when I'm with you. My blood runs free and wild when you're near. We're meant for each other, my love." Emotion chokes my throat, my heart slamming against my chest, trying to get out and hold hers.

She does not look away. Her fingers lace through mine, her tips digging into the sweet spot above her heart, her shaky inhale seemingly endless.

"I love you, Drew. I never stopped. It was just the pain of what I thought had happened that held me back. It consumed me. It blocked out everything else in the world. Now that I know the truth, I feel like I can see the sun again. I can breathe again. I can live." She closes her eyes, a single tear slipping down her cheek. "I can love."

Her eyes fly open and lock on mine. "I can love *you*."

Four years.

A bolt of pain shoots through me, paralyzing my heart. She finally trusts me. After all this time, all this heartache, so many years of struggle and hard work, I'm getting what I want.

Her.

Honesty is the best policy, right?

I need to tell her the truth. *My* truth.

But it sticks in my throat, choking me.

"I love you," I rasp, the words pushed out of me so hard the air lifts tendrils of her hair, making them float. She gives me a kiss, her hands tightening around my shoulders, and I hug her back. She loves me. She trusts me.

Those bastards didn't win.

Bzzz.

"Fucking phone," I mutter, actually grateful for a break from Lindsay. the dissonance between our professions of love and my inner turmoil too much. I check the screen. Gentian.

Your suit is out here. The bathroom's clear if you need to shower, he texts.

I make a sound close to a grunt. He's ready to run a presidential campaign single-handed.

Tks, I type back.

And then I'm on top of Lindsay, my hands on her neck, my thighs on either side of her hips, my chest rubbing against her breasts, the friction of skin against skin generating an impulsive energy that fuels me.

"I am dangerously close to having your father not only fire me from managing security for you, but if he finds me in your bedroom, my ass will be kicked thoroughly."

She pinches the ass in question. "You could totally beat my daddy in a cage fight."

I kiss her and laugh at the same time.

"Not something I really want to test out, Lindsay," I say, pulling myself off her, grateful to have a distraction. Sliding into my shorts and sweaty t-shirt, I watch as she crawls under the covers, her gorgeous shoulders peeking out over the top of the sheet.

I sigh.

I plant my hands on my hips and think for a few seconds. My phone says it's 5:21 a.m. To be safe, I should get out of her bedroom by six. Meeting's at seven, here at The Grove in the senator's office, so it's a fifty-fifty chance whether he'll be here in person.

I need ten minutes to shower. Ten to shave.

Fuck it.

I grab my shorts and pull them down. The waistband snags on something hard.

I'm naked in three seconds, slithering under the sheets as Lindsay squeals.

I silence her with a kiss.

A Harmless Little Ruse

"I have time for one more."

"One more what?" she asks, batting her eyelashes with mock innocence.

"Oh, you need instructions? Let me show you," I murmur as I split her legs open with my hands, burying myself in a place where the past doesn't exist.

And where her pleasure *is* my present.

CHAPTER ELEVEN

"**D**on't try to bullshit me, Drew. I know exactly what you were doing yesterday when you cornered Blaine Maisri and punched him. Convenient there's no video." Harry's voice drops to a deadly whisper. We're in his home office, Anya quietly leaving us alone with a reminder that Harry has a call with the party chairman in ten minutes.

It's 7:02 a.m.

"If that's all you'd done, we wouldn't be in this meeting. But you dragged my innocent daughter into it, damn it. Made her faint from the stress. Just when we had our first success with reputation rehabilitation."

I can taste his innocent daughter on my tonsils.

"Now there's a video clip of her pointing through an open Exit door, eyes wide and fearful like Bambi after his mother was shot, complete with a fainting spell. If we don't spin this carefully, the media's going to resurrect her scandal."

I bite my tongue. And inner lip. And curl my fingers into fists.

"We're covered," I assure him.

"I didn't ask whether we were covered." His look is designed to make me cower. It fails. "I am telling you that you fucked up."

I just look at him.

"I know why you punched him, Drew."

Wasn't expecting that.

"You acknowledge what he's done? You know he's one of Lindsay's rapists?" I can't keep the shock out of my response.

Harry ages ten years in two seconds.

"Jesus, Drew. You're sure?" He looks away. His shoulders sag.

This isn't the first time he's been told this bit of information. I can tell.

"Absolutely sure. I was there," I say through gritted teeth.

"They told me..." He weakens, grabbing the edge of his desk for support. "They said it was *possible*. Not a certainty."

"'They' who?"

"The video analysts. Other advisors." Like who, I wonder. Marshall? Victoria? Those "LB Incident" people from the meeting with Lindsay?

He gives me a bleak-eyed look. "Why didn't you tell me?"

"Why didn't you *ask*?"

"Ask *you*?"

"Ask Lindsay, for starters. And yes, me. We're the victims." I hate that word. A flash of the psychologist who helped me after the attacks hits my brain like a missile strike. I shove the image away.

Victims.

"We got reports from her doctors on the Island, but they said her information wasn't reliable. It came through a drug fog."

"Then let me make the truth abundantly clear to you, *sir*. Blaine Maisri was, without doubt, one of the people who raped and tortured your daughter."

He bares his teeth at me, like an angry stray dog.

"I'm supporting his bid for my old House seat. I've endorsed his campaign. You tell me this *now*?"

"Don't play dumb, Harry. It doesn't suit you."

He's pale, his shoulders rising with each breath, chest moving fast. "Fuck you."

My eyes narrow instinctively, examining him. He's not lying.

But he's not telling the truth, either.

"Do you," he says tightly, "have any idea how thin the ice you're skating on really is, Drew? Blaine Maisri has connections you cannot fathom." His eyes bore into me. I don't flinch. I don't move.

I stare back. "Like Nolan Corning?"

No reaction.

"And those connections are more important than your daughter," I challenge.

It's not a question.

"No." I expect more anger in his answer. "But pissing off Blaine and the people behind him does nothing but put Lindsay in more danger."

More danger.

"He's been texting her."

Harry blinks in surprise. "More texts?"

"Yes. Threats. Pictures."

"You traced them directly to him?"

"No."

"Then you've proven nothing, which means we can *do* nothing."

"Not true."

"You have to act within the law, Drew. This is my presidency at stake. The election year is a weird one. Once I'm nominated as the party's candidate in the general election, it's smooth sailing."

"How do you know?"

He shoots me a dry look.

"I know."

"But that assurance isn't there through these early stages?"

"No."

"Then this may very well involve Nolan Corning. He has a reputation for being cut-throat, Harry."

"So do I, Drew."

"What if he's behind what happened to Lindsay?"

"You think Nolan Corning convinced three college frat boys in your circle to do what they did to Lindsay out of a sense of...competition? Are you insane, Drew?"

"I am considering all possibilities."

"You sound like one of those '9/11 was an inside job' nutters."

"Why won't you even consider the idea?"

Silence.

He's a cipher. I won't get more out of him. Time to cut off the chit chat.

"Blaine and whoever's behind him are using Lindsay against you. Always have."

An imperceptible shiver runs through him. "You mean they're using her reputation against me."

I almost say it.

Almost.

"No, Harry." I drop my voice. "They're using *her*. You know what happened with the brake lines. They're trying to paint her as a crazy. It's all a lie. But once they do that, they'll try to taint you by association. We need to cut this off now. The fish rots from the head."

"I know you're not referring to me."

"Of course not. I'm talking about whoever is pulling Blaine Maisri's puppet strings. Whoever's been pulling them for four years. It can't have escaped your attention that Blaine's rise has been meteoric. He's my age and he's a state senator. He's barely old enough to even *be* a U.S. Representative, constitutionally."

Tap tap tap.

It's Marshall, one of the PR handlers for Lindsay that Harry hired last week. *Last week.*

She's been home barely a week.

He doesn't make eye contact with me.

My hackles go up.

"Senator? A word?"

Harry frowns at me, then turns, giving Marshall his full attention. The guy's eyes dart to me, then down to a newspaper in his hand.

I can't see the picture on it, but I immediately know it's bad. Whatever's on that cover, a shitstorm's about to be unleashed.

Harry pivots and tosses the newspaper on the table between us.

I'm on the cover.

I am the shitstorm.

My sharp inhale feels like someone's shoved an icicle down my throat.

He's going to ask me to explain. Explain why that photo shows me punching Blaine. Explain why that photo captures the moment I unleashed on the guy.

And explain why it's clear I was aiming for him.

No other man is in the frame.

I compose my thoughts even as they race at breakneck speed.

And then he beats me to it.

"You're fired."

CHAPTER TWELVE

I nod, blinking, like this is unexpected.

It's not.

"You understand, of course," he says in a tone that makes it clear I'd damn well better not argue. "We can still spin this so we save Lindsay's reputation. The 'attacker' slipped out a second before. You were shoved by the perpetrator and off-balance. Whatever we say, the focus will be on Lindsay. Not you. I won't have my daughter's barely salvageable reputation affected in any way by you, Drew. Not any more."

"I'll take myself off the case." My mouth is numb. I am speaking through nine layers of glue.

"No."

I look at him. He's imposing as fuck, but I'm strangely detached. Not intimidated a bit. This is about reality and facts. I moved from the asset to the liability column with one newspaper photo. I get it. I do.

"You're *fired*. Officially. We're about to make a very public announcement declaring as much. I'm sure you understand it's nothing personal. This is about damage control. Read the headline."

I look down.

Deranged Ex-boyfriend Stalks Presidential Candidate's Daughter.

"Those *assholes*."

"They may be assholes, but they outsmarted you, Drew. I can't have them contaminate Lindsay. Thank God, nothing in that article implicates her, but -- "

Contaminate?

"Don't you see what they're doing, Harry? Are you kidding me? They're isolating you. Making you fire me. You're handing them exactly what they want!"

"I don't care about their agenda. Only my own. And you know I have to do this."

"Keep Gentian. He's my best guy. And if you're going to hire someone -- "

"I've already called Mark Paulson. Left a message."

A tiny tendril of hope shoots through me.

"Good. Mark's great."

"Stay away from him. I don't want anyone to know you two are associated."

"He works for me."

"Not any more. He's spinning off his own company as we speak. On the record – he's officially disgusted and shocked by your behavior."

I grind my teeth. Damn it.

"He's James Thornberg's grandson. That legacy will rub off on him. Give him legitimacy. Might even help me with polling. A loose mental association between Thornberg and me could help with this mess."

This mess.

I am this mess.

"And Lindsay?"

"What about her?"

"You know how hard this is for her, Harry. I've been able to help her with -- "

"You mean how you're helping her in her bedroom?"

If he said anything else – *anything* else – about Lindsay, I wouldn't look away. But even I can't maintain eye contact with the father of the woman I'm sleeping with as he calls me out for it.

I have limits, too.

"Damn it, Drew. Every worst-case scenario is coming true. Marshall warned me this was a possibility."

I jolt. "Marshall?" Marshall won't make eye contact, but he's also not cowering. The guy won't even look at me.

"He said you weren't ready. And he was right."

"Who in the hell are you to decide whether I can do a security job or not?" I make it clear with the way my eyes check him out that this pasty, overweight, pompous overachiever is the last person qualified to judge me.

"He called it, Drew."

"I want to hear it from him."

Beady eyes, narrow and angry, meet mine. "This isn't personal," Marshall says in a monotone. "The fact that you can't understand that confirms that firing you is the right choice, Foster. That's how the game works."

"Protecting Lindsay isn't a game."

"I never said that. But the presidential race *is* a game – a game of strategy. You don't fit in. Not with your personal vendetta against one of the key players."

"Key players? Blaine's a *key player*?"

"He's more important as a strategic piece than you are. Consider yourself lucky Harry's found a way to still use Paulson."

"I don't give a shit about that, Marshall. This isn't about billable security hours or money or friendship. The stakes are higher!"

"That's right. They are. A presidency is at stake here, and we're not going to let you compromise that because you had some kind of argument years ago with Blaine Maisri over a woman," Marshall snaps back, going for the jugular. A bitter smile makes his lips twitch.

The fucker is *enjoying* this.

I am thunderstruck.

I've seriously underestimated him.

"A *what*?"

"Blaine told me all about it. He dated Lindsay. So did you. You've become unhinged since she came back. You aren't thinking straight."

Harry's watching us carefully, though I can tell his attention is split. He knows this is bullshit. I calculate quickly.

One of two pieces of information is true:

1) Marshall is on Blaine's side and somehow Harry doesn't realize it

2) Marshall has been kept out of the loop on all the details from four years ago.

Both can't be true.

And both are dangerous as hell.

If I have to pick one, though, number two is easier to deal with.

Number one is the choice I'm most worried about.

I ignore Marshall and turn to Harry. "You know the truth about Blaine Maisri, Harry. Is this really your final decision?"

His look doesn't waver. Unlike Marshall, he doesn't avoid my eyes. "Already been made. Mark Paulson will call you shortly. Hand over all your codes, passwords, *everything*, to be changed over to new. Stay away, Drew. Stay far away. It's about press coverage and appearance." Harry grabs my arm and pulls me aside. He's not rough. In fact, the move is smooth, like he knows he can touch me this way.

I yank my arm out of his grasp.

He needs to know he *can't*.

Harry gives Marshall a look. The guy leaves the room, shaking his head, on his phone before the doorknob clicks with a finality that feels like a guillotine blade.

"I mean it, Drew. Don't come near her. No covert mission. No unauthorized security on her. I'll consider that stalking and have you prosecuted," Harry insists.

"How well do you know Marshall?"

The question catches him off guard. "What?"

"How well do you know him?" I stare at the back of the door.

"Since college days. We were in the same fraternity." His eyes narrow. "Why? Do you know something about him *I* need to know?"

This is why Harry has gotten as far as he has. A lesser man would become angry and defensive with my question. Not Harry.

He's all matter-of-fact

"No, but this doesn't make sense."

"You're clearly upset, and I understand -- "

"No. Harry. This. Doesn't. Make. Sense. My guys cleared the security angle. No one had a reason to take that picture in that exact moment."

He rolls his eyes. "So you *did* plan this."

"Yes." Might as well admit it. What do I have to lose? "And that makes the picture in the newspaper more troubling. Marshall's the one who came to you with it?"

"He's my reputation management specialist. He's the one who *would*."

"Fine. But how close is he to Blaine's camp? For God's sake, Harry, you know that story about Blaine dating Lindsay is bullshit."

"He took her to a dance when they were in high school, Drew. We have photos somewhere in an album at home. So does Blaine."

I trawl my memory. I was a senior the year Lindsay was a freshman. We weren't dating yet. "You're basing my alleged stalker status on that pretense? That bullshit?"

"It doesn't take much, Drew," he says sadly, surprising me. The guy is cool as can be, always in a logical frame of mind, ever calculating. "It's all about appearance."

"You appear to be easy to manipulate, Harry. Marshall's playing you."

"You think he's a plant?" I expect him to be angry, but he gets to the point.

"Don't know. Getting rid of me makes sense on the surface," I say, conceding the point. "Now that it's all public and you're worried about *appearances*. Your team can spin this."

"Already has. It was an accident."

"But if Blaine's lying and claiming this is a grudge match over Lindsay, it just thrusts her into the limelight more."

"Shit," he grumbles.

"Right. Look. I'll stay away – publicly."

"Drew." My name is a stretched-out growl.

"But there's no fucking way I'm leaving her alone."

"You don't trust Paulson and Gentian? Your own guys?" His eyebrow quirks, as if to say, *And you let them protect my daughter?*

"I'd trust them with the president."

His eyebrows raise. "Good to know."

"But I don't trust anyone but me with Lindsay."

Any other man would roll his eyes. Harry just blinks. "You sound like a lovesick puppy."

I say nothing.

"You can't tail her. You can't be caught on camera."

"Not a problem."

111

"If Blaine's somehow part of all this – and I still have my doubts – then whoever schemed to get that punch on camera is a step ahead of you."

"Parallel to."

"Excuse me?"

"Not a step ahead – they're running parallel to me."

"You're splitting hairs."

"I'm being precise."

"I don't authorize any of this."

"You don't have to."

"And what about Lindsay?" he asks.

"What about me?"

We both pivot to find her in the doorway, dressed for a run, hair pulled back in a ponytail, face freshly scrubbed.

She's glaring at Marshall, who looks at her like she's an annoying little girl interrupting Daddy's work as they both walk into the room, Lindsay edging him aside.

Before anyone can answer, she looks at the newspaper. Her eyes go wide and she whispers a curse word.

"What is going on, Daddy?"

Interesting *who* she chooses to ask.

"Your security detail was caught on camera punching a state rep," Marshall answers.

"Are you my daddy?" she asks, her voice full of sugar but her eyes bleeding poison all over him. "If so, my mom has a lot to answer for."

"Lindsay," Harry barks. I can tell he's horrified – and trying not to laugh. So am I.

"I'd like an answer from the man in charge," she says, pandering to Harry, who knows it.

And smiles.

"Drew was caught on camera punching Blaine Maisri. We're taking him off your security detail."

"No!" she gasps. I can't tell if she's more upset that I was caught on camera or that I'm being removed.

"Paulson and Gentian can do a capable job of managing you. Their techniques will be *different*," he says, casting a pointed look my way.

Lindsay blushes.

Huh. Didn't know she could be embarrassed like that.

It's cute. And if I weren't consumed by being fired from the most important security detail of my life, I'd find it a little hot, too.

"I never liked Drew being in charge anyhow, Daddy," she announces, eyes suddenly hooded. Contempt shoots out of her eyeballs as she gives me a look her old friend Mandy could have easily extended. It's condescending, haughty, and designed to convince Marshall that she doesn't want me.

It's a ruse.

"I told you that from day one."

Day one. Lindsay's been home for a handful of days. So much has happened.

Too much has happened.

And I know it's only the beginning.

CHAPTER THIRTEEN

"I'd like a word with you," I say to Lindsay.

"No!" Harry and Marshall are in stereo.

"In private, away from the windows and anyone with a camera. That too stalkerish for you?" My words are addressed to Harry and Marshall, who look at each other as they decide. Not Lindsay.

She ignores them, grabs my arm, and yanks me angrily into the kitchen, where Connie is arranging fruit and cheese on a plate. Her head bobs up and she grabs the tray, busily walking down the hall to Harry's office. People tend to skedaddle when tempers are close to blowing.

"I haven't even had my first coffee of the day and you get yourself *fired*?" Lindsay hisses.

I pull my biceps out of reach and turn away, opening a cabinet.

"What are you doing?" she asks, furious.

"Looking for the coffee beans. I can't have this conversation right now. Not when the taste of you is still on the tip of my tongue and your father just confronted me about sleeping with you."

Not to mention the scarves set me the fuck up.

"Daddy *what*?"

I shrug.

"You have the most robotic range of emotions I've ever seen in a man, Drew."

I find the coffee beans, pour some in the grinder, and before I press the grind button, I lean into her and whisper, "You didn't think so when we were naked and in bed an hour ago."

BZZZZZZZZZ.

She can't argue as a florid blush fills her gorgeous face. I know she wants caffeine as much as I need a distraction. Harry and Marshall aren't going to give us much time together. Loose tongues can be found in any politician's household, no matter how careful security is with background checks and ongoing evaluations.

Trust me.

I know that all too well.

How in the hell did someone snap that photo of me punching Blaine yesterday?

Anya appears, her face pale, eyes narrowed into glittering blue slits that make it clear I'm not on her list of favorite people.

Not sure I ever was.

"You okay, Lindsay?" she shouts over the grinder, the ever-present folders in her arms, her face lined with exhaustion. Anya's been part of the background of Harwell Bosworth's political world for years. And then I remember.

Back in the day – way back, before she came to work for Harry – she worked for Nolan Corning.

"I'm fine," Lindsay shouts back. "Just trying to talk to Drew."

"Looks like he's not cooperating." She glares at me.

I glare back.

"I'm making her coffee!" I smirk.

Anya's perfectly manicured finger points to a spot over my shoulder. I turn.

A giant silver carafe full of coffee is on the counter behind me.

Lindsay rolls her eyes.

"I make better coffee than that mud."

"Hey!" Connie's offended voice comes up behind me. "That is organic Fair Trade 'mud' made from beans produced in a Guatemalan coffee plantation that Mrs. Bosworth has supported for years through her humanitarian efforts."

"Fired," Lindsay whispers to herself, blinking hard, looking at me askance.

I cock one eyebrow. "Let's grab coffee and some privacy."

"Privacy? Here?" She snags a mug next to the big coffee dispenser and makes a cup, her palms encircling the china, her sigh full of so much stress. Earbuds dangle from around her neck, the little nubs brushing against her nipples outside her t-shirt. She sips, her eyelids down, then she looks up at me.

The sad smile guts me.

"They set me up, Lindsay."

"I know. And Daddy knows it, but he's all about winning. Have to keep up appearances."

"Were you eavesdropping?"

She shakes her head, a wry smile on her lips. "No. I just have the drill memorized. Daddy only has a few plays in his playbook, Drew. And they all revolve around getting elected."

"You know I'm not what the newspaper – that's just a bunch of lies."

"Of course I know that!" A few sips later and she's pensive. No one interrupts us, but in the background I hear phones ringing, copy machines and printers churning, the muffled busy-ness of a politician who has just declared his candidacy for president.

"You sure?" Every nerve in me is like a candle wick, on fire and burning down the line.

She squares her shoulders, the ear buds dropping, her pony tail bouncing slightly. "Yes. I trust you." Looking around the room, she takes the chance, stepping into my space. My heat.

My body.

Her hands go to the nape of my neck as she leans in, hot breath against my jaw, and whispers, "I trust you. I know that now. Nothing you do could make me doubt you. *Nothing*."

I go cold.

All these years I've chased her trust. The relentless pursuit of control over my body, my space, my work, my reputation, has culminated in this moment. I've served in combat, killed people, saved lives, nursed wounds, and put my own broken hull of a body and soul back together with duct tape and grit.

The moment I've been waiting for is now.

And all I can do is feel a massive wave of guilt.

Because the man Lindsay finally trusts isn't the person she thinks I am.

Which means she's trusting a lie.

Marshall walks in, gives us a disgusted look, and addresses Lindsay as she pulls out of my arms and retrieves her coffee.

"Your father needs you for a short briefing."

"I'm about to go for a run."

"It'll have to wait."

"You don't control my schedule," she announces, gulping down the rest of the coffee.

She flounces out of the room like it's an Olympic event and she's a gold medalist in Condescension, pointedly going outside for a run.

Leaving me shredded.

CHAPTER FOURTEEN

"Drew! Good to see you, though the circumstances sound intense." Dr. Salma Diamante's office is California Fresh, with turquoise walls, creamy sandy-colored carpets, and seashell-themed design elements conveying the feel of the beach. It's serene, stark --

And all too familiar.

"Dr. Diamante." I sit in my normal spot. Habit. You spend nearly two years coming for once-a-week sessions and you pick a spot that's safe. You pick the same damn seat every week because that's one less decision you have to make.

When your mind is like Swiss cheese at the center of a napalm tornado, the less complexity, the better.

"You booked a two-hour session, I see," she comments, eyes intent, studying me calmly. Her body language is relaxed.

She has all the time in the world.

Good. She'll need it for my problem.

"Yes. Figured I'd get it all out of the way in two hours and then I won't have to come back."

She doesn't laugh.

Instead, she takes a deep breath, her way of controlling her responses. Kind eyes meet mine. They're the color of deep brown, the shade a mixture like German Shepherd's fur, reddish-gold flickers along the edges. Salma is my mother's age, but tall and thin. If she were a teenager, I'd call her lanky.

She's in her fifties, so I won't.

Her hair is pulled back in a severe bun, streaked with gray here and there. No makeup. No manicure. I know very little about her. Does she have kids? Grandkids? A husband?

Hell, a wife?

Don't know. I came here for more than a hundred sessions and all the information is a one-way street.

That's the point of therapy, though.

Right?

"Drew." My name rings out in the small room. A seagull makes a strangled sound outside the window. "Drew, why don't you start with the newspaper?"

"The newspaper?" I repeat dumbly.

She nudges her chin toward the coffee table.

Huh.

I'm on the front page.

"You don't have to guess, then," I say with a sigh, shifting in the overstuffed chair. There's a box of tissues on an end table to my right, and another, larger box on the coffee table between us.

Not that I ever needed a tissue.

Two years, no crying.

They ought to give out awards for that.

"I don't have all the details. Why don't you tell me?"

I predict she'll shift her position next, just enough to trigger some primal instinct in me to fill the silence.

She does.

I stay quiet.

I stay quiet until it eats away at me.

The anticipation, that is.

Not the anticipation of what's coming next in this session, this room, this conversation.

But the burning anticipation of how close my own secrets are to being revealed to the world.

Lindsay's not the only one with a past she wants to bury. But she trusts me now, and I can't live with myself if I keep the truth from her.

That's a more brutal form of betrayal.

"I'm back together with Lindsay." The words aren't the first ones I want to say. But they'll have to do.

Salma doesn't really react. Her eyes stay on mine, the skin underneath crinkling up, a non-reactive reaction.

The look encourages me to talk more.

"They let her come home. They made her stay at that mental institution for four years. Harry Bosworth called me and hired my company to be her security detail. Yesterday,

Blaine appeared at Harry's big announcement. It sent Lindsay into a tailspin."

"Only Lindsay?"

I give a half shrug and say nothing.

"How does it feel? To be around her again?"

I can't talk. The room fills with air, like a balloon being inflated. My eyeballs float in my head, my scalp rising up to meet the ceiling. My fists close and my thighs tense.

I have no control over my body's reaction to Salma's question.

"Great," I rasp. It's hard to choke out the word.

I tell the truth.

"You still love her."

Notice how that's not a question?

"Yes."

"And when you saw Blaine near her?"

"I was prepared to kill him with my bare hands right there."

She looks at the newspaper. "You showed remarkable restraint, then."

"I should get a medal."

She gives me a somber smile. "You have quite a few already, Drew. Do you need more?"

I can't really react to that. So I don't.

She breaks the silence.

"You punched him."

"Yes."

"Wanted to hurt him."

"Yes."

"For revenge."

"Yes."

"Who were you avenging?"

"What?" My brow tightens.

"You or Lindsay?"

The feeling that the room is growing extends, the walls stretching like taffy, the floor dropping into a pit, the space dark and blindingly white at the same time.

I know what she's really asking.

"Both of us."

"The unfairness of the sexual assault would make any person experience a triggering episode, Drew, upon seeing their attacker."

My lips are numb.

"But the level of sexual assault that *you* experienced four years ago from those three men, combined with your combat experiences, make your encounter with Blaine all the more traumatic."

She said it.

It's out there.

I haven't told anyone other than Salma. Emergency room doctors, my parents, my sister, and probably some NSA officers know what those bastards did to me that night.

And that's *it*.

Salma blinks rapidly. It's a sign she's trying to approach me carefully. Finally, she asks, "Lindsay still doesn't know the full truth from four years ago?"

"No."

I can say that loud and clear.

Because the word is screaming like a bass drum in my head. *No. No. No. No. No.*

NO.

This is the part where I admit I'm a hypocrite. I'm a Grade-A bastard. I hold Lindsay to a double standard. Where I have one set of rules for the rest of the world and a very different set for me.

I do.

I know I do.

Because I want Lindsay to confess to me and trust in me and lean on me and let me protect her and love her.

But I'm a liar.

I lie to her every day, every second, every breath.

Every kiss.

Salma shifts her weight again, blinking slowly, just waiting. The first seven sessions we had together, years ago, involved nothing but silence.

Mine and hers.

It took seven hours for me to realize she wasn't going away. That she wouldn't judge.

Didn't help that I had no choice. My commanding officer threatened me if I didn't go to therapy.

For seven sessions I stared at any object in the room and tried to ignore the screaming in my veins.

And on the eighth hour, I broke. I gave in.

I talked.

And didn't stop talking for nearly a hundred sessions.

"How do you feel about that, Drew?"

Ah, there it is. That old chestnut. *How do you feel about that, Drew?* Salma has asked me that countless times, and I've answered it, mostly with the truth. *Mostly.* Sometimes I lie at first, but the truth eventually wiggles its way in.

Now? Not so sure what's about to come out of me.

"I feel like Lindsay's safety is my priority. She's struggling enough with her own baggage from four years ago. I don't need to add mine to the load."

"You are very protective of her."

"Of course I am. There's no way those assholes are hurting her again."

"Is there a serious chance of that happening?"

"Yes," I bark, looking away. I rub one eye, then sigh. "They're directly threatening her with text messages and covert communications."

Her eyebrows arch. "I see. Including the picture of you that you mentioned in your voice mail."

"I can't tell her." I plant my elbows on my knees and rake my hair with both sets of fingers, head down, fighting nausea. "Not yet."

Not ever.

"Can't, or won't?"

"Does the difference matter?"

"You tell me, Drew." She smooths her hands over her skirt, making it cover her knees, and leans forward, elbows on her thigh bones. The move is slick and designed to be unobtrusive, but for some reason it reminds me of Lindsay.

Everything reminds me of Lindsay.

"Can't. Won't. Both. Look, Salma, if I try to tell her what happened to me that night, she'll – we'll – I – damn it." I feel this getting away from me. My hand rips through my hair. It's shaking so hard I feel my teeth chatter.

She waits me out.

"It'll complicate everything," I finally choke out.

"The truth usually does. And then it simplifies."

I'm losing it. I'm losing it and *fast*. Blood that normally pulses through me at a steady pace is roaring in fits and starts, making my chest heave and sputter. All that skin covering muscle and bone feels like it's floating in outer space, like gravity stopped working.

The world telescopes and pinpricks, then it expands and widens until I'm living in a funhouse mirror.

And I'm the clown.

"Drew," Salma says. "The longer you wait, the harder this will be. I understand your concerns for Lindsay's mental health, but they wouldn't have brought her home from the facility she was in if they didn't think she was emotionally strong enough to handle whatever the world throws at her."

Salma has no idea how much that is.

"I -- "

"And you deserve to clear the air. To own your experience. Until you can talk with her, I'm not sure you're going to be able to move on." She's using shorthand. We don't have to go through all the layers of the past because Salma and I have processed what happened. Jargon and shortcuts mean we can get to the heart of the matter fast.

Too fast.

"Move on from what? Lindsay?"

"Move on from your victimhood."

"I hate that word. Victim. Let's use the word *survivor*."

Warrior.

She nods slowly. "It's a better word. It is. But you were a victim before you were a survivor, and we need to honor that phase."

Victim.

My fingers dig into the arms of the chair I'm in. The pain radiates into my knuckles and I welcome it. Fuck. It was a mistake to come here. I don't have time to dig up my past.

My future is in jeopardy.

And Lindsay's present is nothing *but* danger.

"I shouldn't be here." I feel a trickle of sweat run down the back of my neck. My underarms are soaked, like I've run a 10K.

"Drew. *Drew*." Salma says my name firmly. "We don't have to talk about anything. Not at all."

She goes silent.

My heart beats. And beats. And *beats*, each thump for Lindsay.

Who is at home now, confused, being watched by whoever Paulson assigned to her, all my texts to her unanswered since I saw her yesterday morning in the kitchen. Who knows what Harry has her security team doing now. I know they've shut me out. That much is certain.

She slipped one through to me somehow, on Jane's phone.

It just says, *Shore. Tonight. Eight.*

Clarity hits me between the eyes, the feeling so intense it's tangible. I pinch the bridge of my nose as if a mosquito just stung me.

"No. I do have to talk. I'm here because even I know this is destabilizing. I love Lindsay more than life itself and I'm afraid I'm fucking this up already."

She glances at the newspaper. "I see."

"That punch got me fired. Harry Bosworth took me off the case protecting Lindsay. We were just getting closer again," I say, my voice filled with regret.

"Intimately close?" Her voice is so neutral she might as well be screaming. The dichotomy makes no sense, but nothing makes sense right now.

"Yes."

"And how was that?"

I shoot her a speculative look. "I'm not a kiss-and-tell kind of guy."

She laughs, the sound genuine. I've surprised her. "I'm not looking for lurid details, Drew. I'm asking about your psychological health."

"What does sex have to do with that?"

Her turn to give me an incredulous look.

My laugh surprises me. It's deep and rough, and sounds like it's coming from outside my body. "Sex was good. Great, actually. Especially when she doesn't steal my gun afterwards."

Peering intently, Salma asks, "Is that a euphemism for something sexual?"

"I wish."

Her eyebrows go up.

"It's a long story."

"You booked two hours." Her comment comes with a small smile.

I give her one back and cross my arms over my chest. I'm playing games. I shouldn't. The mess with Lindsay is a tornado filled with flaming pieces of my soul, my career, my life. All of it spirals, pushed by forces beyond my control. I hate it.

I hate not being in charge.

But I'm here because it's the right place for me to be. Paulson nudged me, and being fired was all I needed to call and get in with Salma.

I'm here.

I should be productive with my time.

"I wouldn't be here if it weren't important," I start.

"Of course. Reconnecting with Lindsay is important."

"And destabilizing," I add.

"You've used that word twice now," Salma notes.

I shrug. "You introduced me to it. It's a good word. Fits how I feel."

She nods and stays silent.

"Four years ago," I start, my mouth going dry. I cough, clearing it. "Those bastards drugged me. Made me watch. And then..."

I close my eyes.

It's like the last four years didn't happen. I'm back in that room, at that party in a rented beach house. We were all buddies from high school. Blaine, John and Stellan had been on the lacrosse team with me. I'd known them since middle school. Wasn't a fan of Blaine and John, but they were okay. Good for partying and having fun. Lindsay was with Tara, Mandy, and Jenna, and Jane was there, shy, against one wall in her own little category. Alcohol flowed.

I was graduating from West Point in a few weeks, home for some family event. The Saturday night party was a fluke. Lindsay's dad was running for re-election to the U.S. senate, and earlier that day he'd talked to me about my future. Said he could help me get in with the Secret Service.

Now I am more powerful than any Secret Service agent.

But for all the wrong reasons.

I'd been drinking. So had Lindsay, but we'd both agreed to a three-drink limit. She was still underage and always worried about how her actions would reflect on her father. I didn't want to be hungover for my flight back to school the next day.

None of it mattered. We'd been so careful, and not one iota of it mattered.

"Would you like to do some guided imagery, Drew? What do you see when you close your eyes?"

"I see failure."

"What does failure look like?"

My own face flashes before my eyes.

"Me." I know from being in therapy that the first answer isn't always true. Damned if it doesn't feel like it, though.

"What color is it?"

"Blue, purple and red," I blurt out, surprised.

"The color of Lindsay's scarves," Salma says quietly.

I jolt. My heart canters in my chest like a skittish horse.

"Have you tried to imagine her face as you tell her?"

"Try?" I open my eyes. "I don't have to try. I see it every day, every second. Not a moment goes by that I don't imagine how much she'd be disgusted if she knew what really happened that night." My fists tighten again. Any equanimity or clarity I was working toward is now long gone.

"She's smarter than that. She loves you. She wouldn't -- "

"*Loves* me? Lindsay can barely trust me. We're sleeping together but it feels so weird. Like I'm part of some game. A ruse. I'm just..." My throat tightens. My pulse feels like it's jumping rope.

"You're together but you think she's manipulating you?"

"I know she is."

"Then why are you with her?"

"Why do iron shavings attach themselves to magnets?"

"You're hardly an inanimate element, Drew. You are a sentient, grown man who can make choices."

"Lindsay *is* a choice," I say, my voice gruff.

"But you're terrified to lose her if you tell her what Blaine, John and Stellan did to *you* that night."

I look at her. "It's not just about losing Lindsay. I'm ashamed, okay? I'm filled with residual shame and disgust. If that were all, I wouldn't be here. If word ever got out about what they did to me, my business would die. People hire me to protect them. Image is everything. Having it known that the owner of a security company was once drugged and -- " My throat goes dry again, but I have to say the words.

Have to.

Not because Salma wants me to, but because some part of me drives forward, knowing I can't get over this until I own it.

" -- and they...abused me like that."

She nods once, slowly, a form of praise that I wish I could absorb.

"And doing it while I couldn't fight back, after forcing me to watch them defile my girlfriend is a career ender in my field." I have to change the subject. Deflect. Disengage. Talk about anything but *me*.

"Which worries you more? Losing Lindsay or losing your reputation and business?"

I snort. "I don't need my business. Between my inheritance after Mom and Dad died and some side work I could always have, I'm fine financially."

"So it's losing Lindsay that terrifies you."

"I wouldn't say *terrifies*."

She doesn't respond.

Terrify. Fuck that. I'm not terrified at the thought that Lindsay would find out about what those fucking beasts did. I'm *not*.

"Drew. You were hospitalized for weeks as a result of the damage they inflicted on you."

I start to shake. It comes from within, vibrating out of my ribs, feeding into my arms and legs.

I can't control it.

I can't control anything.

"You've been so focused on Lindsay and her trauma that I think we need to process your view of her reaction. When she finds out -- "

"She'll only find out if I tell her."

And hell, *no*, I'm not telling her.

"When you're ready, that will be a major step toward healing. For both of you."

My eyes go unfocused. The shaking doesn't stop. Rage stored in my bones tries to work its way out. When I first started coming to see Salma, I needed to run out of the room. I felt too raw, too exposed, to be around her. She tolerated it. Encouraged me to leave and compose myself.

Took months to feel safe.

Took nearly two years to be done.

Here I am, back in the same place.

But different.

Does Lindsay feel like this? Home for a week, already mired in scandal. Except this time, I'm the source of the scandal. Those assholes set me up, and now Harry's listening to all the wrong advisers.

For all the "right" reasons.

"I don't have time for the emotional fallout of having what happened to me revealed to Lindsay. It's another complicating factor. Right now, there's already too much going on. Her safety is paramount. Sifting through the past has to wait."

"Sifting through the past may be the most important way you can keep her safe, Drew."

I close my eyes again.

Damn it.

Now I remember why I kept coming back to Salma.

Because she's *right*.

"They're threatening her. Directly. Cut her brake lines and nearly caused a crash. Now Blaine's sniffing around her at her father's declaration rally. Hell, he weaseled his way into getting Harry to endorse him for Harry's old House seat. They text threats to her and make it look like it's coming from a phone she bought. It's all manipulated, calculated, and it's impervious. We can't figure out how they're doing it. Someone on the inside is helping them. They're sharks circling to find the right time to bite. I cannot introduce yet another element of complexity to this situation."

"You're not introducing it. You're identifying it. Acknowledging it. By doing so, you help to remove the power the past has over both you and Lindsay."

"Power?" I lean forward, shoving a hand through my hair again. "They have no power over me. I've systematically stripped their influence out of my life."

"You wouldn't be sitting here if that were true, Drew." She taps the newspaper. "And they wouldn't have been able to do this."

All I can do is blink. I freeze, as if I'm trapped in my body, paralyzed. Blood rushes to my head, away from my heart, flowing into my fingers and toes.

My chest stops moving.

The world stops.

"Look," I say, the word coming out of my mouth with so much effort. Instead of thinking in sentences, I'm working with syllables here, one at a time, chained together to form words that link with other words to make my thoughts come out. I inhale, then exhale, and say, "If that is true, then four years were wasted."

"Why do you think that?" she asks kindly.

"Because I spent all this time getting ready for Lindsay. Making sure she'd always be safe."

"Are you sure it was Lindsay you were protecting?"

"What?" Anger pours through me like my skin is just a mold, and fury fills it.

"I don't think you were only trying to make the world safe for Lindsay. You were working to make it safe for you, too."

"Of course I was," I scoff. "I *am*," I stress. The air conditioning clicks on, making me jerk. The sound surprises me, the deep whine of the system hurting my ears. I'm holding my breath and I let it out, my respiration inconsistent, the feeling that I can't catch my breath becoming overpowering.

"Not as a byproduct, Drew."

I frown. "Lindsay's safety is always more important than my own. I'd die for her."

Salma nods. "And that is admirable, but who would die for you?"

She might as well throw a brick at my face.

Because suddenly, my mother and father's faces fill my mind. How they looked at the viewing at their funeral.

How their brakes failed.

Oh, God. They victims, too. How far does all of this go?

Did my parents die because of *me*? Because of some strange fixation Blaine, Stellan and John have on destroying my and Lindsay's lives?

Bzzz.

The room makes no sense suddenly, as my emergency phone goes off. Salma glares at my jacket, sitting on the couch.

"You know I have a 'no cell phone' policy, Drew."

"I know. It's turned off. That's my Code Red phone. It only goes off when there's a life-or-death emergency."

Fuck.

I leap up, rifling through the cloth, the pocket edge ripping as I grab the phone and answer.

"Foster," I bark.

"Drew. This is bad." It's Paulson.

"Lindsay?"

"She's fine," he says, but his voice sends a cold ribbon of panic down my spine. "It's you I'm calling about."

"Me? What about me?"

"That guy who works for Bosworth – Marshall. He's claiming he has intelligence that proves *you're* the one sending the threatening texts to Lindsay."

"What? What the hell?"

"I know it's bullshit. But the tracing report got into the hands of Blaine Maisri's camp. They're threatening to leak this to the press. It's one hell of a set-up. We need to do damage control for you."

Damage control.

My entire life is turning into nothing but damage control.

Bzzz.

My phone vibrates in my hand. Incoming text. Salma gives me a look of studied frustration. I know this is sacred space. I know I'm supposed to work on my issues.

Trust me.

I know.

But this situation just went FUBAR and the ante just got upped to the Nth degree.

I ignore Mark as he tries to get my attention, and I look at the text.

Don't play if you can't win, it says.

I go numb.

Another text. It's a video. The picture has the Play symbol in the middle, a frozen image of me, naked, on my side with a mask over my head.

A video.

There's a video of *me* from that night?

"Paulson," I snap. "Full press."

Dead air fills the line.

He hasn't just hung up on me.

Mark's gone to start a series of procedures that threaten to destroy everything I know.

But all in the service of saving Lindsay.

I stare at the texts. Deep breaths come out of me, involuntary, as tumblers in my mind sync, creating an orderly chain reaction.

I know what to do next.

I don't like it, but I know what I have to do.

Then it hits me.

They're sending that video everywhere.

Lindsay. They'll text it to Lindsay next.

Probably already did.

"Drew!" Salma's voice fills with a pleading horror as I stand, striding to the door with purpose. I can't look at her. I am a shell now. Shells hold vulnerable creatures, protecting them from the dangers of the outside world.

I can't be naked and soft. That's for a different part of me, one that can't come out and play right now.

A game, right? We're playing a most dangerous game.

Which means the man who walked into this room cannot be the one who walks out of it.

"I'm fine. Bill me, Salma."

Her face turns red with anger. I watch, wholly detached. Like the good soldier that I am, trained in psychological as well as physical warfare, I can separate feelings from flesh.

I've done it before, so many times that being connected is the exception and not the rule.

It occurs to me that Lindsay does the same.

I can't think about that right now.

"This has nothing to do with money. I'm concerned about dis-regulation in you. You need to stay."

I pause, my hand on the doorknob. There's no turning back now. None. What Paulson is unleashing is the equivalent of starting a nuclear launch sequence. Lindsay isn't the only person with a revenge plan. Mine has been in the making for four years.

A love plan for Lindsay.

A revenge plan for those pieces of shit.

I didn't think both would be initiated at the same time.

But there's only so much I can control in the world, right?

"Salma, what I need to do is find out how to stop the people who are hellbent on destroying my life. I came here to try to sort through everything with Lindsay, but the texts and call I just received show that she's in even more danger than I ever thought. So am I."

"What was that about?"

"I'm being set up. Blaine, Stellan and John are trying to make it look like I'm the one threatening Lindsay."

And a video of what they did to me just appeared.

Her hand moves to her mouth, a gesture of shock, but she's too smooth. Too professional. Salma catches herself, then slowly lowers her hand, bracelets jangling at the wrist. "I see. The newspaper article?"

"And some texts Lindsay received. They've been traced to one of my phones. It's all being done to make me look like I'm unhinged. Like I'm the one who's trying to hurt her. Turn me into a stalker, make Harry look bad for hiring his own daughter's crazy ex...you can put the pieces together. And if they get their way, Lindsay will be left in an unprotected state and her current team will hand her off to the -- " I crack my sentence in half. "No. That can't happen. I have to go and stop them."

That's as emotional and revealing as I can afford to be.

A tingling starts in my knees. It is not unpleasant. Full-body flushes are like a horn on the battlefield in ancient times.

A call to arms.

In a way, I am relieved. Excited, even. While I'm a tactician and a strategist, four years has been too long. Too much planning, not enough action. Too much rumination, not enough motion.

Too much pain.

Not enough pleasure.

An image of Lindsay crashes through me, as if she's entered my bloodstream and strokes me from the inside out. What will she think of me when she finds out? When she views that --

All I want to do is find her. Steal her away. Take her someplace where none of this can touch her.

All I want is peace.

Too bad I have to go through hell to get it.

I leave.

Salma doesn't try to stop me.

Chapter Fifteen

"**S**ilas!" My voice sounds like shrapnel ripping through flesh. I'm on my emergency phone and he's answering before I realize I've shifted to his first name, the soles of my feet digging into the floorboards of my SUV, the unrelenting sun turning the cab of my car into a sauna of retribution and recrimination. The air tastes like regret. "I need your help. Now."

"What do you need, Drew?"

So much for "sir."

"Block texts going to Lindsay's phone. Effective five minutes ago."

"I can block all future texts, but -- "

"Scrub them. Now."

"She has her phone on her, sir – Drew. Too late."

Fuck.

"Where is she?"

Silence.

Silence.

Silence.

"SILAS!"

"She's...er, well, she's asking for you."

Careful what you wish for.

You just might get it.

"Me?" I gasp.

"Yes. We're under strict orders not to have her see you, be seen with you, come within a thousand yards of you, even -- "

"I get the point," I grind out.

"But you know Ms. Bosworth."

My grimace turns to a tight grin.

"Sure do."

"She's insistent."

A lump in my throat makes it hard to swallow.

"What's her mood like, Silas?"

"Her...mood?" He asks the question like he's not sure he heard me right.

"Yes."

"It's, um...she's pretty stoic. Broken record. She just walked over to the senator's office and it looks like she's arguing with her mom and dad."

Lindsay can take on Harry.

Monica? Not so much.

I'm a man of action. I plan and strategize, examine tactics and enact scenarios.

Waiting isn't my style.

"I'm *persona non grata* at The Grove, I assume."

"If it were legal to shoot you on sight, I'm pretty sure Marshall would have ordered the team to do so," Silas replies with a rueful huff.

"I guess I have to see her."

"You guess?"

"I do. I need to see her."

"What's going on? Is there intelligence I haven't seen yet? A viewing of new evidence I missed?"

Oh, is there *ever*.

"This is personal. Between Lindsay and me."

"Understood."

"But it has to do with the texts on her phone. How many people have access to that information?"

He names Paulson, himself, and one techie on the team.

"Scrub those texts and remove the techie."

"I have to clear this with Paulson," Silas insists.

"Then do it." Every word out of my mouth feels like I'm one step closer to death.

"Sir, why are the texts so important?"

As I look out the windshield, the world widens. My hands itch to have Lindsay here, in my arms, her skin under my heated touch, to have her concrete and palpable, able to be grabbed and secured.

Then again, maybe I need her as an anchor.

To keep me from floating away.

"Sir? Drew?" His voice changes, choked with compassion, and it hits me.

He knows.

He saw.

Bzzzzz.

A text from a number I don't know.

Jane gave me a burner phone. Ignore whatever they're telling you. Find me at the shore tonight at 8 p.m. Silas will help.

"Drew?" Silas's voice is back to normal. "Anything else I can do for you?"

"I think I'll do a little night running on the beach later on," I say, testing.

"Good idea. I hear the weather'll be great for it."

Click.

I spend the rest of the day taking care of paperwork, tying up loose ends in my business, chatting with my sister and Facetiming with my toddler nephew.

Because no one can predict what's about to happen next.

Least of all me.

CHAPTER SIXTEEN

"**D**rew, you're nuts." It's nighttime, right before 8 p.m., and Paulson's at the perimeter of The Grove, arguing with me at the shore. Because I know every nook and cranny of the estate's grounds, it's easy to bypass four men at various stations.

Not so easy to get past Mark.

"Don't put me in this position, Foster. Lindsay didn't ask for you. In fact, she's been badmouthing you to everyone she sees." His eyes are hard, but they also plead with me.

Back down, they say.

My eyes transmit a two-word message to him, too.

They're not the same words. Mine start with F and Y.

"That's part of some scheme of hers. C'mon, Mark. It's obvious. She's creating fake distance between us." Not a shred of worry inside me. I know her ruse.

"I don't know what's obvious anymore, Drew." He sighs, the sound loud and frustrated. "I had no desire to be head of security for a presidential candidate's daughter when I said yes to you last month. This is madness. I should be home kicking back beers and being with Carrie."

"You can always quit."

He makes a sound of disgust. It happens to be the sound of loyalty, too.

"Like that's going to happen. You fished my girlfriend out of an underground bunker using old sewer pipes before she could have her limbs removed by a crazed drug lord with an amputee fetish. That's the definition of owing you."

"When you put it that way...yeah. You absolutely owe me."

His mouth goes tight.

I cross my arms over my chest and stare him down.

"If I let you in, not only will Harry fire me, he'll remove the company from covering Lindsay. Your time's limited anyhow. Secret Service is stepping in more and more. They're harder to evade."

"Right." I know I have a narrow window of time. "I just need to see her tonight. That's it. I'll be done after this."

His sharp look doesn't faze me. "That's it?"

I feign innocence.

"That's it."

"I don't believe you."

"Believe what you want. I don't care. I do care whether you trust me."

"I trust you to do something stupid."

"That's a start."

His voice goes cold with anger, teeth clenched, arms flexing as our friendship gets overridden by his sense of duty.

"I'm not fucking around, Drew. Your presence compromises her. Those guys are after *you* as much as they are after her. You're literally luring them to her. What are you thinking?" You would think his anger would upset me, but just the opposite happens. I'm pleased. When he's this protective of Lindsay, I know he's vigilant. I know that anyone who tries to hurt her will have to go through Paulson, too.

"They texted me today."

He closes his eyes, then runs a hand over the back of his neck, tension bleeding off him. "Of course they did. What'd they say?"

"'*Don't play if you can't win*'," I recite, the words like burrs on my tongue.

"Assholes. That's just a taunt."

"And a promise."

"A promise of what?"

"That they'll follow through. I have to talk to Lindsay. I think I know what's about to happen next and I need to warn her."

"Care to share with her head of security? Not that you're exactly forthcoming with important information." He is pissed. The double meaning is clear.

He *knows*. He knows about that video.

I don't care, actually.

Part of the truth is all he needs.

I ignore the barb. Can't deal with it. "They're going to invent some charitable cause for her. She'll be sent to work with the homeless in Haiti, or with a literacy program in Appalachia, or to restore hurricane damage in Guatemala. Whatever the story, it'll be designed to get her out of the limelight and for all the attention to die down." I say this with impatience, and Mark crosses his arms over his chest like he has all the time in the world.

He knows I'm in a rush.

"You're the focus of attention on the news so far, Drew. Not her. And her attackers are tormenting you now, too. Exposing you."

Ignore ignore ignore.

"But it taints Harry by default." I barrel on. "The media's being nice to her today, but give it two or three more days and the worm will turn. And getting her out of sight means she'll have less security. Any company other than mine that handles her security can be compromised. Probably already has."

"You think Blaine, John and Stellan have that much power?"

"Not them, no. But the puppetmaster behind them? Yes. We need to figure out who's controlling them. That should be the number one mission, aside from protecting Lindsay. Harry's too wrapped up in his campaign and getting bad advice to realize it."

Mark looks at the house, the moonlight bouncing off the gentle waves, illuminating the windows facing the ocean. He's a man with two opposing duties. Loyalty to me. A promise to Harry.

Which one does he break?

Mark's phone goes off. He looks at a text.

"Lindsay's insisting on being driven to her friend Jane's house in two hours." His fingers fly on the glass screen, then he taps with finality and catches my eye. "Don't even think about following her."

Two hours. I have two hours, then.

"You're not my commanding officer, Paulson."

"And I'm not your employee anymore, Foster."

"We're at a standoff, then. And you know how standoffs work. Motivation always wins."

"Motivation often kills, too."

"I need to talk to her, Mark. She's at risk. " Appealing to reason generally works with him.

He's on his phone again, his face screwed up into an intense grimace. "You can't get caught. Lindsay isn't just a senator's daughter now. She's about to be under Secret Service protection as a presidential candidate's family member. You know the difference."

"Which is why I have to talk to her *now*."

Urgency and patience don't go together well, but somehow I manage to harness both in this conversation.

"You know where Jane lives?"

"Apartment downtown, on the water. Yeah."

"No," he corrects me. "That's her mom's place. Jane's in some middle-rent apartment complex by the I-5." He gives me an address. "I didn't tell you that."

"You also didn't give me two hours."

"Didn't do that, either." He looks pointedly near a cluster of bushes at the edge of shore. I see a suspicious blonde ponytail poke up among the greenery.

"This conversation never happened." I mouth the words *Thank you*.

"*You* never happened."

And with that, one of my best friends walks away, leaving me by the ocean. I have a new mission.

I don't exist.

"Drew?"

Maybe I do.

Her voice is tentative, so hesitant it's like she's peeling my skin off, one strip at a time.

"Drew. I saw the video. Oh, God, Drew."

CHAPTER SEVENTEEN

E ver walk on stilts? That's how it feels as I make my way
across the sand toward the cluster of shoreline brush that
dots the beach. The carefully landscaped grounds of The
Grove have to give way to untamed nature at some point.

That line is here.

Right between our bodies.

There's no moon tonight, just a cloudy grey sky that
doesn't leave witnesses. No one can see us unless they're
trying. I get the feeling Mark's given the rest of the team
explicit orders to give us space. I also know my time is
limited.

Whatever's about to happen needs to be swift.

Bold.

Complete.

I don't say anything as I stop a few feet from her, waiting.
None of this is within my authority. Lindsay calls all the shots.

"I saw." The wind picks up her words and carries them
out over the ocean, the words licked by salt water, diffused
into the enormity, made part of the water and sent to parts
unknown, where dragons live.

"You did." I don't ask.

"I saw enough. I didn't need to watch the whole thing –
oh, Drew. Why didn't you tell me?"

And there it is. Four years of anticipating that question.

And it's happening now.

I open my mouth to answer and nothing comes out. I
widen my eyes to see her better and my vision pinpricks. I flex
my hands to reach for her and I freeze.

I can't.

I can't.

I can't because four years ago, I couldn't move. All I could do was watch.

And for the last four years all I've done is acted.

But I've acted alone.

"Don't answer that," she says quickly, berating herself. Not me.

"I – you – you deserve an answer, Lindsay."

"I deserve more than an answer."

My heart stops, waiting in my chest for orders.

"Drew, we deserve so much more. Who knew? I didn't. You really couldn't stop them. Worse – they made you watch. And then they hurt you, too." She laughs. It's the sound of chimes on the wind, the sweet release of relief, the mellifluous tone of someone who has given herself permission to feel whatever she wants.

It's the sound of fresh rain and old love.

It's the sound of hope.

I brace myself for the inevitable. Salma warned me that Lindsay might ask too much of me. Might try to extract more than I could give. I always said I could handle whatever she threw at me.

Salma's wise.

"I'm sorry," I say, my mouth numb.

"Don't ever say that again. Now that I know the truth."

Now that I know the truth.

"Don't you see?" She's smiling. *Smiling.* Why the fuck is she laughing and smiling? Anger and seething I expect.

Not this.

Not *ever* this.

"See what?"

"You, Drew. *You* make sense to me." Her palm flattens over her heart, fingers tickling the base of her throat. "That was the hardest part about what happened to me. The fact that I couldn't reconcile the man I knew with the man who acted the way you did. You weren't the same person. But now I understand." Shallow breaths turn deep as her chest rises and falls, the sound of her inhales and exhales mimicking the ocean behind her.

Her eyes are my moon and stars. "I am so, so sorry for what they did to you." Even without moonlight, I can see the shine of tears pooling in her eyes. "But knowing the whole truth makes me so relieved."

Relieved?

"And pissed."

That's more like it.

"We're – you're – I -- " A ragged breath turns Lindsay raw and real as a breeze blows her hair across her face, the stray strands not tied up in her pony tail catching in her mouth, shading her eyes for a moment. "For four years I felt like this damaged little thing. The fucked up little girl who no one trusted. Because I – because you didn't care."

"Lindsay." Her name is a vow coming out of my heart, into my throat. "That's not true."

"I know it's not. I *know*," she whispers intensely, stepping toward me, closing the gap. "I know. And this sounds so awful – so wretched – but I have to say it. And if you hate me for it for the rest of my life, then I'm sorry, Drew."

"Say it." I brace myself.

"I -- " She hesitates, swallowing hard, the night air stifling, smashing me into myself, turning me inward.

I reach out and rest my fingertips on her elbows. "Say it," I whisper, destroyed by touching her, feeling unworthy.

"Now we're equals," she says, chin up, eyes blazing.

"Equals?" I choke out. Not what I expected to hear.

"I'm not the only one they hurt. We have a bond that is deeper than I ever imagined. We're linked in ways that are unfathomable," she explains, tilting her head as she studies my reaction.

A loud puff of air pours out of me. I've been holding my breath.

"This isn't how I want to be bonded to you. Not from shared pain."

"It's not my choice, either. But it happened. It's there. It will always be there, and those assholes are blind to what they *really* did to us."

"Blind to what?"

"To the fact that they thought they were taking our power away." A look of marvel washes over her face. "Don't you see, Drew? If I could go back four years ago, I'd stop what happened."

"So would I! In a fucking heartbeat." As if on cue, my heart smacks up against my ribs like it's trying to escape and go backwards in time to fight.

"But we can't."

I grab her arms, hard, as if I'm pulling the kernel of what she's saying out of her. I don't understand her words. This is the most honest conversation I've ever had with a person, and I can't believe it. "Why are you saying all this, Lindsay? I failed you. *I failed you.*"

"No. *They* failed me. They failed humanity. You're human, Drew. You *couldn't* stop them. I spent all those years thinking you wouldn't stop them, but you *couldn't.*"

"I can now. I *will* now."

"Yes. We can now. *We.* Us. Together. We're stronger together than we ever were apart. That's the secret, Drew. This is who we are now." Her hand reaches for my heart, pressing. "They thought they were isolating us, taking away our power. But we're more than that. And I'm not alone."

I grab her hand and hold it like it's the key to every mystery in the world. "You were never alone. Not in here." I push her hand against my chest.

"I wanted to believe that. Even when every piece of evidence showed the opposite, I couldn't let go of loving you."

"Thank you." My stomach unclenches. She slides her hands to my waist and pulls in for an embrace.

"You're shaking," she mutters into my shirt.

I ignore the comment. She's not wrong. "When did you become so wise?" I ask.

"Not wise."

"Do you have any idea how hard I've worked to hide what they did to me? Especially from you?" I expect her to look at me, but she stays in my arms.

Thank God.

"You never had to. You never have to hide who you are from me, Drew."

"What they did to us isn't who we are, Lindsay."

She nods, the movement warm and sweet.

"Suddenly, revenge feels more immediate," she mutters into my chest. "More possible. But for different reasons and with different goals."

"What do you mean?" I ask, pretty sure I know the answer. My body is still on edge from this entire, surreal conversation. Lindsay knows the whole truth now. All of it.

And she's relieved? She feels *closer* to me? I'm *not* rejected?

I don't know what to feel. So much of the last four years has been about preparing myself for the chance at redemption. Too much energy has been focused on hiding what happened to me. My biggest fears haven't come true.

Aside from being set up by Stellan, Blaine and John in the media, getting fired by Harry, and having them use hackers to make it look like I'm a deranged stalker, the day's going damn well.

"I trust you completely. Wholly. And that means we can work together," she says. Her grip on me tightens. Her heart skitters against my ribs, and one hand slides down my back, resting at the base of my spine. She's warm and soft, and the way she sinks into me is comforting.

The body cannot lie.

"You said you had a plan for revenge," I venture, rubbing her back, breathing slowly against her. All the adrenaline that coursed through me minutes ago like rain in a drought starts to recede, replaced by a protective streak that's bigger than before, if that's possible.

She loves me.

In spite of what she knows, she *trusts* me.

No. Scratch that.

Because she knows the truth, she trusts me even more.

"I do." She chuckles. "It involves video."

I tense. "More video...of me?"

"No. Me."

I frown and pull back, holding her at arm's length. "Explain. I don't want *more* video of you anywhere, Lindsay."

"What if I told you my darknet hacker friend got their hands on a video of that night, where they – where Stellan and – where..." She clears her throat and squares her shoulders. "Where they aren't wearing masks?"

"That video exists?" I'm skeptical. "You've seen it?"

"Yes." The evil grin that spreads across her face makes my insides ripple. It's not a smile.

147

It's a vow.

"I don't want another video of them attacking you to become public. Not even if it means taking them down."

"You will when you see this one."

"Damn it, Lindsay, I don't want to see it, and I don't want anyone else to, either!" I shout, ready to explode.

"It's proof, Drew." As her voice drops, she sounds exactly like her mother. Cunning, sharp, and in for the kill. "*Proof.* We'll destroy them. It's what I've wanted."

"What *we've* wanted," I say reluctantly. Although it's true, I hate the idea that she has to face media scrutiny again.

Has to be exposed like that.

"There's something else," she says, watching me. Her eyes narrow. "What is it? What are you worried about?"

"If you spread that video, they'll spread mine." The truth makes my stomach roil.

"Who says they haven't already?"

I close my eyes, the truth of her question turning my mind into a blank wall, a white canvas, a black hole.

A rustling sound, louder than the wind on leaves, catches my attention. Instinct draws my hand to my weapon, which I'm not wearing. Lindsay halts. I press one finger to my lips and urge her with my hands, carefully guiding us both into a crouch, shoulders hunched. Who's out there? Gentian? One of Harry's Secret Service guys?

"Harry, I don't understand why we need to be on the beach. This godforsaken wind does so much damage to my skin. You know that!"

Monica.

"Is that my mom?" Lindsay whispers, horrified. "What is she doing outside? She hates walking on sand."

Given that the Bosworths have lived in this oceanfront estate for all of Lindsay's life, the contradiction makes no sense.

Then again, when you understand Monica's all about appearances, it fits.

"We need privacy, Monica." Harry's hand slips around her waist, the gesture intimate. Lindsay stops moving, staring at the sight with a gentle interest that breaks my heart. Harry and Monica have always struck me as a political couple, their marriage a business arrangement.

The idea that there's any love between them – other than the love of power – is surprising.

Monica rests her head on Harry's shoulder and laughs. "Oh, you. Mr. President."

"Not yet." Harry's low voice carries on the wind. Lindsay's watching him with rapt attention, her eyes bouncing from her mother to her father. "We've got a long way to go."

I have to close my eyes and fight the memory of my own parents, so different. Mom and Dad loved each other with a public reverence I found annoying as a teen.

When I look at Lindsay, I feel the same intensity my parents had for each other.

"Can't be any longer than the road we've already traveled, Harry. We have to spin this Drew mess," Monica says.

Lindsay cuts away to me, mouthing *Drew mess?*

I shrug. I stroke her arm as she leans into me, her warmth calming. Soothing. I'm still ten thousand live wires on the inside, though the current's turned down. Too much input. I need time to process everything, and hour by hour my situation worsens.

Lindsay smiles at me.

Or not.

"I've taken care of it," Harry replies.

"Nolan Corning is three steps ahead of you, Harry. He'll use Drew against us."

Nolan Corning. There's that damn name again.

"Let him try. Drew's being targeted. It's all a witch hunt. I had to fire him, but I won't throw him under a bus."

"Why not?" Monica asks. Lindsay's amusement drains out of her face, lips tight.

"Oh, please, Monica. You're not a stupid woman. It's plain he's in love with Lindsay and she loves him back."

"What does Lindsay know about love, Harry? When did you become so soft?" Her tone is chiding, feminine and alluring. "I'm worried she'll get hurt again." Monica's voice carries a self-righteous note. "He hurt her so much, Harry. I can't bear to watch that again."

Lindsay looks like she's ready to unleash claws on her mother. Or hug her. Could go either way. Shock ripples through her face as Monica's words of concern for Lindsay sink in.

"I made a terrible mistake last week, Monica. I have to unendorse Blaine."

"What? Why? You can't be viewed as a waffler. That's political suicide."

"Not waffling. Just...remember that briefing on the incident? About who the men in the masks were?"

Monica goes quiet.

"Yes," she finally says, her voice filled with skepticism.

"I have confirmation it's true."

A sharp intake of breath ends with a breathy squeal of outrage. "That little shit! Blaine really was in on it? Nolan never said a word."

Nolan? What the hell is going on here? Why does Harry's party rival continue to come up?

Lindsay makes a snorting sound. Monica and Harry turn.

"We can't let them see us," I hiss, pulling her closer. Lindsay loses her footing and crashes sideways into a big batch of ground brush, squealing slightly as her leg disappears in the greenery.

The click of multiple weapons sighted on us, then the flurry of bodies moving not-so-covertly fills the space around us. I thrust my hands in the air, red laser dots covering my shirt like crooked constellations.

"I'm clear! No weapon!" I shout, knowing exactly how protocol works. Getting shot isn't high on my list of priorities right now. Two agents surround Harry, two work on me, patting me down until they're satisfied.

"He's fine. Not a threat," Harry announces.

Monica snorts just like Lindsay did a moment ago. "What are you doing here, Drew?" Monica shouts, her voice a hard knife blade. "Haven't you done enough damage?"

The look Lindsay gives me says, *I'm sorry.*

"He's being an ass, Daddy. Following me here while I was on a run." She points to her earbuds. "Listening to some Jane's Addiction." She stresses the word *Jane.*

Jane.

Right.

"Escort him off the grounds," Harry says in a monotone, as if telling his personal assistant to hang the dry cleaning on the back of his office door. I'm no one. Nothing.

Not worth emotion.

It hits me.

That's a good thing.

Because when you don't elicit an emotional response from people, what are you?

Invisible.

I'm perp-marched off the grounds, where I find Mark Paulson leaning against the main gate, shaking his head slowly.

"Someone located your car." He nods to a black SUV. "They'll take you to it." He sighs. "You don't know when to quit, do you?"

"Quit?" I purse my lips and shake my head. "I'm sorry. I don't understand."

"We're on the same side, Drew."

"I know."

"She's still going to Jane's place tonight."

I grin. "I know."

And with that, I get a nice escort back to my car, courtesy of the United States government.

CHAPTER EIGHTEEN

G ated apartment complexes are a complete joke. Lindsay's out of her SUV, escorted by Silas to Jane's apartment, and I'm watching the entire thing from a chaise longue next to the apartment complex pool, being chatted up by a senior citizen named Phyllis who thinks I'm the new pool guy.

Five minutes later, I'm checking out the broken pool pump using a back entrance to Jane's apartment. Nice old Phyllis wanders off to make me cookies. I won't ever eat a single snickerdoodle, but it made her leave.

Jane lives on the first floor. Could she be any stupider? What single woman chooses a garden apartment? I make a mental note to tell Anya that her daughter needs to put personal safety at a higher priority.

Scratch that.

No, I don't.

Because I don't exist.

If I don't exist, I can't pick the lock on her back door in ten seconds flat, and if I don't exist I can't slide into her apartment and hide in the bathtub while Lindsay and Jane chat in her tiny galley kitchen, each holding a wine cooler and sharing a plate of chicken wings.

And if I don't exist, I can't wait her out.

Good thing I don't exist.

That leaky shower head sure does exist, though. I wait them out, hoping Lindsay still has a bladder the size of a pea. We joked about it for years, road trips dominated by bathroom stops.

By the time she finally comes into the bathroom and locks the door, my hair is soaked, and there's a cold line of wet cloth running from the nape of my neck down my ass crack.

I wait until she's vulnerable.

Slowly, with agonizing care, I peel back the shower curtain and look for her, ready to shush her.

Except she's not on the toilet.

She's in the far corner of the bathroom, smirking, fully clothed and giving me a once-over look that makes me swell.

"Took you long enough."

And then her mouth is on mine. We're hungry for each other's touch and taste. She's all grapes and sour apple, with a sweet 'n sour scent lingering as our tongues tangle, her hands sliding under my wet shirt to find my back, the heat of her palms making me groan.

We don't even have to say it. Being back together, being free together with the secrets of the past poured out between us leaves me pulsing with anticipation.

With *need.*

Lindsay feels it, too.

"What's with the ninja costume?" she asks, laughing against my jaw.

"Ninja pool man," I whisper, biting her earlobe.

Her hand cups me, making me hiss, the promise too much. "Don't get me going. Not when we can't do anything about it." She ignores me and begins stroking me over my pants, touching me in unspeakable ways.

At least, I can't speak right now.

"Jane left. We're alone. I can finish anything you start, Drew. I can't believe how much I want you."

That's all I need to hear.

"Not here, though," I warn. The fact that Jane made herself scarce tells me she's close to Lindsay, which is a double-edged sword. I want Lindsay to have friends, a confidante. On the other hand, the more people know about my actions, the more at risk Lindsay is. Jane's trustworthy.

To the extent that anyone is.

"Where?" she gasps as I circle her nipple with my thumb, making it peak, the reaction arousing. She sighs, a breathy sound that pushes against my jaw as I kiss her again. I can't get enough of her. I need to be in her, need to make her know how much I want her, how incomplete I am without her near me.

A cheap apartment bathtub in an unsecured location isn't cutting it.

"Can't do my place," I whisper. "I'm sure I'm being watched."

"Same with my house," she hisses as she reaches down the front of my pants and very expertly wraps her fingers around my hard shaft.

All logic shatters into a thousand soft pieces of groaning bliss.

"Jesus, Lindsay, don't do that!"

She strokes once, twice.

I start to shake and grab her wrist, hard.

"Not like this," I insist.

She lets go of me and in a flash, pulls off her panties, throwing them casually aside. They catch on the light switch.

"It's right here, right now, or nowhere, Drew." Hands on her hips, she gives me a jaunty smile. Bold and powerful, eager and bright, she's suddenly the Lindsay I knew four years ago.

I can't say no.

Hell. What man could?

And who would want to?

We're on the floor in seconds, her legs wrapped around me, mouth hard and urgent against mine. We're seconds away from just riding each other when I stop, shaking, and pull away.

"What's wrong?" she asks.

"I don't want to just have a quick fuck."

Her laugh is unexpected. "You don't? Are you sure you're a human male, Drew?" The sardonic tone makes me wince. *You'll regret this tomorrow*, that tone says.

"I meant I don't want *just* that."

"When did I ever say that was all we were going to do?" she whispers, licking the edge of my ear as she sits up, her hand on my ass. "Let's take what we can get and find room for more after."

Oh, God. Everything happens so fast. We're locked in a bathroom in Jane's apartment, half naked and full-blown crazy, panting and hot and aroused and hard and then I'm in her, all slick warm velvet and cream, her thighs tight on my hips, her fingernails scratching my back over my shirt, her warm, wet breath urging me as I slide into home.

Over and over and over, her hips arching up to catch me, Lindsay takes without mercy. I'm flying, flipping her so I get better traction, pumping hard as she begs for more, her body tensing, her orgasm seconds away.

As my hips move and she meets me every inch of the way, momentum builds, my breath in my ears and her scent all over me, our naked skin sliding and slipping. Our bodies are in tandem as she moans my name, her neck stretched and taut, her fingers digging into me as she clenches and releases into the abyss that has no name, no face, no label.

Just pure energy.

I can't hold back, my cock jerking as my thighs shake, her gorgeous body under mine, turning me on and making me a live, naked wire as I come hard, muffling my shout in her hair, my pulse so fast it's like I've skipped dimensions. Every move she makes incites me, excites me, makes me want her more.

"I can't get enough of you," she moans in my ear right before she kisses me, our teeth crashing, lips moving with a hunger that I mirror.

I'm still coming, incapable of speech, my hands on her breasts, her ass, her hips – I want it all – and then we're both twitching and panting, my head spinning, and Lindsay laughs so hard I fall out of her.

Evicted.

She's half propped up against the bathtub, her skirt around her waist, the back of her hair a rat's nest and she's hooting, giggling so hard she makes an adorable snorting sound.

Which means this is the perfect time to give her my gun.

No, not the flesh one I just fired into her.

A real one.

She crab walks, scrambling to get away from me as I hand her the tiny pistol.

"What the fuck, Drew? Is this some military custom I don't know about? Sleep with your girlfriend and give her a gun or something?"

Girlfriend.

All the air in my body whooshes out. White spots dot my vision, then clear to give me the truest vision of Lindsay I've ever experienced. We're ragged and sweaty, soaked in each other's musk and half dressed, on Jane's bathroom floor, as a group of enemies seek to destroy us.

And I've never been happier.

She is radiant.

I press the tiny pistol into her palm as I kiss her deeply.

"You need this. Just in case. And you need something even more important."

This is when I pull out my syringe. I came prepared.

Her eyes bug out.

"What the hell, Drew? My mom speculated you might be on drugs, but -- "

I show her the microchip.

Now she pulls away from me.

"What the hell is *that*?" The mood is gone.

"A microchip."

"You're the Terminator, aren't you? A cyborg from the future. This explains so much." She's rambling and starts to stand, searching for her panties. I point to the light switch.

"Why are you so focused on time travel, Lindsay?" I stand, too. I'm faster at getting dressed, and by the time she makes eye contact, I have the syringe with the chip in my hands, ready to explain.

"Because right now, I want to be anywhere, any time, but here. Now. What the hell, Drew?" She looks at the gun in her hand, then pings to the syringe in mine. "What is this? You want to..."

"Microchip you."

"I'm not a pet!"

There are so many replies to that one. I smartly hold them all back and just look at her. I lick my upper lip and taste her.

"This is simple. Your dad is making all the wrong decisions."

Bang bang bang.

We both jump and I almost drop the chip, but catch it at the last second.

"Ms. Bosworth?" It's Silas, from the outside door. "We need to get you home."

What he's really saying is, *Get the fuck out of there, Drew.*

"We don't have much time," I say tersely. "I need to insert this in you." I pull out the alcohol swab and grab her wrist.

"*In* me?" She snatches her hand back.

"Yes."

"I have an 'insert one item per day' limit with you, Drew." She shoots me a smug smile, but she's creeped out.

"Not today."

She just blinks, the truth of what I'm saying slowly sinking in, her cheeks going red.

"You're not kidding."

"No."

"You think I'm in that kind of danger? So much danger that I need to be chipped so you can track me in case they – in the event of a -- "

"Yes."

"Is that why you just slept with me?"

Bang bang bang.

This is all too much, too fast, too jumbled and full. Emotion and action don't mix for me. They just don't. You act on instinct and override fear to get the target to safety. Sometimes I'm the target. Most of the time, it's someone else.

You don't *feel* for the target, though.

And the target never has feelings for *you*.

But this is different.

The stakes are higher.

The stakes are *everything*.

"I slept with you because I can't keep my hands and heart off you, Lindsay. I want to chip you so I never have to stop touching you and loving you."

Her neck snaps back with shock, anger melting into desperate love. "Oh, God. It really is that bad."

I give her a look that says it is.

She deserves the truth.

"You cannot trust anyone. Not a single soul," I say, holding out my hand. She puts her shaking palm in mine and squeezes.

"Not even Jane?" she asks.

I don't reply.

Because I don't know.

Then I drop to my knees at her feet.

"Again?" she gasps. "Now really isn't the time for -- "

Bang bang bang. "Ms. Bosworth!"

"I'll be there in a minute, Silas!" she shouts.

"I'm not going down on you, Lindsay. I'm looking for the best place to plant the chip," I explain. Just under the ankle bone? No.

I grab her hand again, pinching the fleshy web between her thumb and index finger. One swipe with the alcohol wipe, then jab.

"Ow!" Her other hand is on my shoulder, digging in, but she doesn't move. Doesn't jerk away. Acceptance on her part surprises me, but she's always been smart. Quick. She gets it.

I wish she didn't have to.

"This is so surreal, Drew," she whispers. "It's like Find My iPhone, only now it's Find My Lindsay."

Exactly. That's the whole point. "Everything about the last week has been surreal, Lindsay. Welcome to my reality."

"I want to live in your reality with you," she says as I throw on a small Band-Aid over the fresh cut. Looking down, she rubs my hair. I look up. "I hate that I've spent the last four years thinking you didn't love me. That you betrayed me."

"That's exactly what they want to do, Lindsay. Distort reality. They want everyone to think that lies are true and the truth is a lie."

"How the hell do we win?"

Bzzzz. My phone.

I know it's Silas.

"Answer the door, Lindsay. Let Silas in." I grab her and give her a swift, fierce kiss, then nudge her towards the door. She looks back at me, so many questions in her eyes, but she nods and does as she's told.

Gentian appears in the hallway as I leave the bathroom. I realize I have no idea what Lindsay did with the pistol I gave her. Maybe she stored it in her bra?

Can't think about her breasts right now.

No.

"Foster, you're out of your mind." He is seething. "You could do time in federal prison for all this."

"It's a fucking set-up, Gentian."

"I know that. So what are you doing here? Get out. Go away. Hide. Leave the country, Drew."

I look over his shoulder, down the dim hallway, to where Lindsay is searching through her purse. She finds a compact and checks herself in the mirror, lips red with kisses, hair a mess.

"No way. I can't leave her."

"You'll leave her if you end up in prison, Drew."

"I have enough contacts in the system to avoid that, Silas. I'm being framed. With enough time and investigation, we can out the truth and -- "

"Listen to yourself." His voice is low and hard. Silas has never talked to me in this tone before. Then again, I'm not his boss anymore. "I say this as a friend, Drew. You sound like some naive conspiracy theory nutcase on a cable channel series. You know damn well the people after you and Lindsay can make you disappear. Or worse. You need to hide."

"If I hide, Lindsay comes with me."

His hair curls as he runs an angry hand through the space over his left ear, then rubs his mouth. "Then you'll have a manhunt unlike any other with you as the target. A presidential candidate's daughter being kidnapped by her stalker ex-boyfriend?"

"That's not -- "

"That is exactly how the press will spin this. Senator Bosworth, too. The whole damn machine goes into damage control and you become the scapegoat. It's so obvious. Jesus, Drew. Mark told me you were being unreasonable, but I didn't think *you* of all people could be so stupid!"

His words cannot sink in. They can't. No matter how right he is, I can't leave her.

"Let me take her back to The Grove. Give you time to sort this out," he says.

I've told no one about the microchip. At least there's that.

"Paulson is personally there right now. Our techies are working on the text issue. They know who Lindsay's darknet contact was when she was at the Island and think there's a link," he adds.

"A link?" Lindsay's voice is high with anxiety. "What do you mean, a link?"

The implications of what Silas is saying hit me. Hard.

"He means that whoever helped you when you were on the Island is potentially behind setting you up for your fingerprints on the brake lines of your car, for buying the phone that texted you threatening messages, and now setting me up."

Her gasp breaks my heart.

Bzzz.

That's Silas's phone. He takes a look, his face hardening. Cold eyes meet mine.

"She needs to get home. Now."

"Please, Drew. What does this mean? What are they doing? My darknet person on the Island helped me to have outside access. To know what the outside world said about me. They didn't -- "

I ignore her words, but walk past Silas and put a comforting arm around her shoulders.

"We need to know who it is," I snap.

Silas gives me a look. "No shit." He pauses. "*Sir*," he adds, his voice bitter.

I turn to Lindsay. "We need to know who it is."

Her face goes slack. "I don't know who my informant was."

I hold my breath. Pretty sure she's doing the same.

This is a standoff.

I break it. I have to believe her.

I kiss Lindsay's temple. God, she still smells like us, like me, a faint whiff of my own musk in her hair. "Silas will take you home. Mark's there. He's right. I'm a liability to you right now. If they're after me, too, then being with you ups the danger for you."

Years of living with other people telling her what to do for purposes bigger than herself makes Lindsay remarkably accepting. "Fine," she says, resigned. Her ankle rubs against mine.

Heat rises through me from toes to crown.

At least I can track her electronically.

That's the only reason I'm willing to let her go.

A Harmless Little Ruse

We're brief. A quick kiss, an *I love you*, and the last thing I see is Lindsay's back, Silas's hand on her elbow, and then Jane's front door shuts quickly.

I escape out the patio door. The scent of snickerdoodles fills the air as I creep past one of the apartments and find my way home.

CHAPTER NINETEEN

The sound of a law enforcement or military team coming to your house for a raid has a distinct racket. Years of training has honed my hearing, my ability to catch a raid seconds before it actually happens one of the soft skills that set me apart during my combat tours.

Unfortunately, that skill doesn't translate when it comes to being the target of a raid.

And that's exactly what I am right now, as uniformed officers carrying assault rifles kick in my front and back doors and swarm my apartment.

Cacophony never seems chaotic in the moment. It rolls out in nanoseconds, achingly slow, blurred lines and confusion on a parallel timeline with the rest of the world.

The crack of the door shooting inward, then another, are close enough to gunshots to make me jump out of bed, completely naked, with my gun in my hand already. Safety off.

Shoot to kill.

Then black cloth and metal glints, sunlight and skin, flesh and angry, cold eyes. My name, barked in serial by a bunch of men and women who not only don't know me, but don't give a shit about anything other than my compliance. They are here to subdue me, to take me away, to check off a box that says the good guys won and the bad guy is in his place.

I don't know what I've done.

They won't tell me.

The gun in my hand, though, changes their calculus.

In the movies, action heroes like Jason Bourne can outsmart a flock of highly trained Special Ops soldiers and take down a crowd of ten.

My limit is six.

And whatever branch of law enforcement has crashed my apartment brought what feels like two hundred elephants, all standing on tiptoes on my kidneys.

In other words, my shoulder's just been wrenched out of the socket by someone zip-tying my wrists together. I see lightning bolts across my vision as the pain sears me.

My rights are barked out to me in a clipped, loud voice, and then I'm hauled on my feet, my gun long gone, my naked body arched forward, vision blurring.

Someone shoves my legs into a pair of orange prison scrub pants, and then I'm perp-walked out my own front door into the back of a van.

Ever shake a bead in a Pringles can?

Yeah. I'm the bead and the van is that can for the twenty-minute drive to the local police station. By the time we arrive, I'm as bruised as an apple being used as a soccer ball.

And through it all, the only thought I have is this:

No fucking way will they win.

It takes Mark less than half an hour to arrive, flashing government credentials that don't mean shit when the people in charge of arresting me don't seem to care about jurisdiction, policy, or the basics of the law itself.

A television blathers on in the corner of the ceiling, the volume too low to hear the newscaster's words, but the closed captioning big and bold.

I'm the star of the show right now, the clip of my arrest being shown over and over, half naked, wearing orange scrub bottoms.

"Submit that video to America's Funniest. You could win the grand prize."

I snort. A bubble of blood shoots out my left nostril.

The news cuts in with a report that Lindsay Bosworth, presidential candidate Senator Harwell "Harry" Bosworth's daughter, will leave today for a humanitarian mission working with Fair Trade coffee growers in Guatemala.

"Sources confirm that Lindsay Bosworth has decided to engage in the Fair Trade coffee project to work on assisting with literacy issues, teaching at the elementary school level. Ms. Bosworth earned a bachelor's degree in education and is

fluent in Spanish, according to Bosworth campaign spokesman Marshall Josephs, and -- "

"No. Oh, God, Harry. No." I groan over the rest of the newscaster's words. This is a joke, right?

No. It's not.

It's dead serious.

Deadly.

Mark lets out a big puff of air, eyes nervous and darting. To someone who doesn't know him, he looks pissed.

A thread of fear tugs inside me, because I do know him.

He's *scared*.

"The scarves set you up one hundred percent, Drew. Now it's your fingerprints on Lindsay's brake lines. You sent the threatening texts to her phone. And Jane's on the record that you broke into her apartment last night -- " He gives me a vicious look. I flinch.

"Jesus, Drew," he groans. "Tell me it's not true."

I stay quiet.

"Fuck, Drew. I don't know if I can undo this."

"I broke in to talk to Lindsay privately! She said Jane disappeared because she knew I was there. Why would Jane lie like that?"

"Don't tell me you seriously just asked that question, Drew." He's looking at me like I'm an imbecile.

"This is worse than I thought."

"We have to figure out who the mole is. Right now, looks like it's Jane."

"Jane." I shake my head, a drop of blood landing on my upper thigh. "No way. She's too clean." Something Lindsay told me about Jane pings in my memory. Computer science. Jane works as a developer for a start-up. Could she be Lindsay's darknet contact?

No way. Jane's not the type.

He reads my mind. "No one's too clean, Drew. You of all people know that. Your best friends turned on you and Lindsay four years ago. What makes you think Jane wouldn't?"

Considering Mark Paulson is the closest thing I have to a best friend, all I can do is stare at him.

165

"I get one phone call," I choke out, coughing so hard blood appears at the corner of my mouth.

"You're exercising that right now?"

"Better late than never."

His face goes slack. "Depending on who, exactly, is orchestrating your arrest, *never* is a distinct possibility." The bones in his face stand out with tension as he whispers, "If they move you out of here, I don't know where they'll take you. The longer we stall, and the more people I add to the chain of information, the better. Once you're out of my sight, I -- " His words break off with a frustrated halt and an angry shrug.

"One phone call. Senator Harwell Bosworth."

"You have brass balls, Drew. Brass fucking balls. The guy's probably behind some of this!"

"I know he's not. And he needs to know that any instructions from any entity to move Lindsay will only endanger her." I recite a number. "That's his private line. Get him on the phone."

Mark hands me his phone. I dial.

"Bosworth."

"Harry, don't hang up."

"You."

One word can sound like a death wish.

"Listen to me. Don't move Lindsay. Any transport puts her at risk," I snap.

"*You* put her at risk, you sick little beast."

"It wasn't me. I'm being set up."

"He said you'd say that."

"Who?"

"Look, Drew. Get help. Go inpatient at a mental hospital, get whatever assistance you need. But stalking Lindsay like this isn't healthy for you. She doesn't love you. She doesn't want you."

I don't take the bait.

"Do not send her to the Island."

His silence confirms what I suspected.

"I know it's not a coffee plantation."

"It's where she needs to be, Drew. No thanks to you. And stop with the death threats against me," he adds, acid in his voice.

"Oh, come on. You don't actually believe that's me, Harry. I can tell you don't."

The sound of a palm rubbing against stubble peppers the phone line. He sighs. "I don't know who has decided to make your life a living hell, Drew, but you pissed off someone very, very high and very, very powerful. I can't save you." His voice tightens, as if he's reconsidering. "Not that I'd want to."

He thinks the line's being monitored.

He's right.

Mark's watching me. Someone taps on the door. He talks in a low voice, buying me time.

"Keep her at The Grove. Paulson and Gentian can keep her safe," I plead. I'm not above begging. Not when it comes to Lindsay.

"That's not the plan."

"Then your plan will kill her, Harry."

"Says the man who sliced her brake lines and threatened and -- "

"You know this is all too convenient, Harry. I didn't do any of that. You're smarter than this. Don't believe their bullshit."

"Besides, it's too late," he says. My heart squeezes.

"What?"

Mark walks back to me, watching closely.

"She's already on her way to the Island."

"Does she know that?"

Silence.

"Fuck, Harry. You can't -- "

"Don't tell me what I can and cannot do. Paulson just left on the helicopter with her."

My heart stops. Just stops, like a deer walking calmly through a dewy dawn, ears perked by a sudden interruption, a pending doom.

I stare at Mark, half-listening, blood starting to boil, mind turning into a tornado. "What?"

"You heard me. Paulson said this was the best approach, so he's escorting her personally. Anya arranged it all."

"Say that again." I can hear my voice drop like a drawbridge.

Mark's brow furrows and he mouths the word, *What?*

I'm staring at Mark. He's staring back.

"Anya arranged for Mark Paulson to transport Lindsay back to the...coffee plantation," he says, annoyed. "Look, I don't have time for -- "

"That's impossible, Harry," I grind out.

"What are you talking about?" His reply is impatient. He's done with me. I'm a bother and if I don't get him to realize what he's doing, more than one person is about to die.

Or worse.

"There's no way Mark Paulson just got on that helicopter to escort Lindsay to the Island."

Mark's mouth opens with shock, then snaps shut.

"I talked to him on a cleared, secure line. Anya arranged it. Hell, I just watched them from across the grounds, climbing aboard the chopper. Don't tell me it's impossible."

"Harry, you just sent her to her death," I shout. I'm shaking uncontrollably, and I can't look at Mark. Who do I trust? Mark made me leave The Grove last night, telling me it was for everyone's good, that I needed to let the dust settle on all the media craziness. Then he hinted I should go to Jane's apartment. Gave me her address. Was that all a lie?

My friends from high school turned on Lindsay and me four years ago.

Is Mark not what he seems, too?

I want to tell him about the microchip, to have Paulson track her...but...

Three officers rush into the room.

"Why?" Harry asks, shaking me out of my whip-fast thoughts. "Why would you say such a thing, Drew?"

"Because," I say slowly, turning on the speaker phone just before they pin my arms behind my back, "Mark Paulson is right here with me."

Paulson's eyes narrow, his eyebrow fixed in place, the only sign of stress a twitch in his jaw muscles.

"He's *what*?" Harry's not faking the incredulity.

"What are you talking about, Drew?" Mark asks, stepping closer to me, then backing up as the three officers make it clear he's next if he doesn't.

"Jesus, is that Mark Paulson? He really is there with you? You're not delusional? Then who the hell just took Lindsay?" Harry shouts into the phone. "Where is my daughter going?"

I'm slammed, cheek down, on the concrete floor and everything fades to a brilliant, familiar red.

The color of one of Lindsay's scarves.

* * *

Read the heart-pounding conclusion of the Harmless trilogy in *A Harmless Little Plan*, found at book retailers everywhere.

ABOUT THE AUTHOR

Meli Raine writes romantic suspense with hot bikers, intense undercover DEA agents, bad boys turned good, and Special Ops heroes -- and the women who love them.

Meli rode her first motorcycle when she was five years old, but she played in the ocean long before that. She lives in New England with her family.

Visit her on Facebook at http://www.facebook.com/meliraine

Join her New Releases and Sales newsletter at: http://eepurl.com/beV0gf

She also writes romantic comedy as Julia Kent, and is half of the co-authoring team for the Diana Seere paranormal shifter romance books.

OTHER BOOKS BY MELI RAINE

Suggested Reading Order

The Breaking Away Series
    Finding Allie
    Chasing Allie
    Keeping Allie

The Coming Home Series
    RETURN
    REVENGE
    REUNION

The Harmless Series
    A Harmless Little Game
    A Harmless Little Ruse
    A Harmless Little Plan

Made in the USA
Columbia, SC
21 October 2018